10636642

DOCTOR · WHO

SnowGlobe 7

DOCTOR·WHO

SnowGlobe 7

MIKE TUCKER

BBC
BOOKS

2 4 6 8 10 9 7 5 3 1

Published in 2008 by BBC Books, an imprint of Ebury Publishing.
Ebury Publishing is a division of the Random House Group Ltd.

Doctor Who is a BBC Wales production for BBC One
Executive Producers: Russell T Davies and Julie Gardner
Series Producer: Phil Collinson

The Random House Group Ltd Reg. No. 954009.
Addresses for companies within the Random House Group can be found at
www.randomhouse.co.uk.

A CIP catalogue record for this book is available from the British Library.

ISBN 978 1 84607 421 9

The Random House Group Limited supports the Forest Stewardship
Council (FSC), the leading international forest certification organisation.
All our titles that are printed on Greenpeace approved FSC certified
paper carry the FSC logo. Our paper procurement policy can be found
at www.rbooks.co.uk/environment

Series Consultant: Justin Richards
Project Editor: Steve Tribe
Cover design by Lee Binding © BBC 2008

Typeset in Albertina and Deviant Strain
Printed and bound in Germany by GGP Media GmbH

For my mum,
for introducing me to good books.
And for Karen,
who seems to like what I write.

Del McAllen shivered, though it had nothing to do with the cold. He twisted his head, the torch mounted on his helmet swinging its beam across the walls of the tunnel that had been roughly hewn from the ice, the pool of light twisting and skittering across the frozen surface. There was something wrong here, something he couldn't quite put his finger on. It was unsettling him.

He shook his head, trying to shake such stupid thoughts from his mind. He was tired, that was all. He was still adjusting to the new country that he had found himself in. It was difficult to believe that only five days ago he'd still been going through the daily routine of his job back in London. Right now he would give anything for the cool calm routine of the British Museum instead of the incompatible extremes of cold and heat that his body was currently trying to cope with.

He tried to bring his mind back to the task in hand, brushing at the frozen tunnel wall with one of his heavy gloves. He cursed softly under his breath. Whoever had designed the thermal suits had never had delicate work in mind. It was like trying to pick your nose with boxing gloves on. He pulled the frost-soaked glove off with his teeth, then ran his bare hand over the cool, wet surface of the wall.

The rock deep underneath the ice was old, ancient, predating the earliest civilisations, and the carvings on its surface were totally unprecedented. Stick-like human figures, gathered around another indistinct shape. Del shivered again. The crude pictures on the wall had invaded his dreams almost every night since the blurred and pixelated digital image had appeared on the screen of his laptop the previous week.

He frowned, dredging at something on the tip of his memory. It was as if the pictures in the rock were somehow stirring something deep in his subconscious, a remembrance of something old and terrible that was now struggling to reach the surface.

He closed his eyes, willing his brain to pull itself together and rationalise the thoughts. Instead, a gruff and booming voice brought him out of his reverie, making him jump. The heavy thermal glove clattered at his feet.

'Careful where you're putting that! And don't forget those power packs when we leave.'

A squat figure clad in lurid orange thermal overalls lumbered down the icy corridor. A dazzling torch beam shone directly into Del's face, forcing him to shade his eyes.

'What you doing taking your gloves off, you daft bugger? Good way to lose a finger or two that is.'

Del squinted as the figure approached. Ed Keely was the works manager in charge of the excavations. A huge bear of a man who had made it plain to Del as soon as the two had met that he didn't like anything that got in the way of the work. And Del was getting in the way big time.

'I wanted to get a proper look,' Del stammered. 'These gloves are too clumsy.'

'Don't need to take your gloves off to look, do you?' Keely pushed past Del, peering in distaste at the intricate carved images. 'Besides, I told you I didn't want you touching anything until we got this tunnel shored up properly, didn't I?' He glared at Del in that supercilious way that he had. The museum curator felt himself flush under the big man's gaze.

'I'm just trying to do my job, Mr Keely…' It was a lame comeback, and he could see Ed Keely drawing breath ready for a withering retort. Fortunately, Del was spared any further embarrassment by a crash from further back down the tunnel. Keely turned angrily.

'What the devil have you managed to drop now you clumsy great ox?'

'Sorry, boss.' A light, delicate voice echoed off the ice and more lights stabbed from the darkness.

Del winced inwardly. The voice belonged to Keely's junior assistant Rwm'dek, and she seemed to get even harsher treatment from the big construction manager than Del did. Rwm'dek appeared out of the gloom, struggling to keep a pile of crates and equipment balanced on an anti-grav sled. 'Sled got a little out of control, lost a couple of boxes off the back.'

Keely glared at her. 'Thought I told you to load it properly. If you've damaged any of our boffin's delicate equipment—'

'It's all right,' Del butted in quickly. 'I'm sure there's no harm done.'

Keely ignored him. 'And where the devil are those flamin' robots I told you to program?'

Rwm'dek nodded back down the corridor. 'They're just coming.'

'Really, well so's old age, and I don't want to spend any more of mine waiting for them to come and do their job. Go and find out what's keeping them.'

Rwm'dek shot Del a quick smile and hurried off back down the corridor.

Keely huffed and shook his head. 'Never ask a Flisk to do a man's job. Should never have let 'em stay if you ask me.'

Del felt himself bristle, but this was an argument he'd already had with Ed Keely and he knew he'd get nowhere with the man's ingrained, outdated, bigoted opinions. Instead, he bit his lip and busied himself with the equipment on the anti-grav sled.

The Flisk had arrived on Earth twenty years earlier, refugees from a stellar cataclysm that had all but wiped out their entire race.

No one had known what to do with them at first. There had been alien contact before, sure enough, but they had always been transitory encounters: sometimes unfriendly like the Sycorax or the Slitheen; sometimes friendly like the Svillia or the Hive of Mooj. The difference was that those visitors had always had somewhere to go back to. The Flisk were asking to stay. For good.

At first the negotiations had gone well. Right up to the point where the Flisk had let slip that they were telepathic. With the revelation that the alien visitors had the ability to read minds, panic swept the world. Leaders on both sides desperately tried to assure the populace that this unique trait proved no threat to privacy or freedom, the Flisk leader even agreeing to a televised meeting with members of the public to try and dispel fears that they could see into the minds of ordinary men and women.

The following twenty years had seen a long and difficult integration of the Flisk refugees into human society. Their seemingly innate genius with all forms of computer programming meant that large numbers of them gained skilled positions in industry across the world, but their telepathic skills, however mild, made them figures of suspicion and distrust for a lot of their co-workers and, with their mottled green-blue skin, the Flisk were an easy target.

A loud, metallic clumping made Del look up. Six tall, gleaming robots marched in unison down the corridor, blocky red serial numbers stamped on their metal chests. Keely and Rwm'dek followed along behind, the Flisk's petite figure dwarfed by the towering steel figures. Even the bulk of the burly construction manager looked small by comparison.

'Right, you lot,' bellowed Keely. 'Madam here has programmed you with your assignments. So get on with them.'

The robots spread out swiftly along the icy corridor, light from housings on their heads playing along the frozen ceiling.

Rwm'dek crossed to Del's side, giving him a shy smile. 'The robots will ensure that there is no chance of the tunnel collapsing whilst we work.'

As Del watched, the robots lowered themselves onto their haunches, steel spikes driving down into the rock of the tunnel floor. At the same time, all six of them raised their arms, placing their metal palms flat against the ice of the tunnel roof. There was a whine of servos and hydraulic motors and a sharp crack from the ice above as the robots took up the strain.

Rwm'dek nodded in satisfaction, her deep brown eyes flickering over the readings of a small scanner on the sleeve of her jacket.

Keely stamped over to her. 'Come on you lazy Flisk, no slacking. No point checking on the remote relays. I want manual confirmation readings from all these mobile pit props before we even bother unpacking the sonic drill… And you,' he glared at Del. 'Don't do *anything* until I tell you it's safe to do it, all right?'

Keely lumbered off towards the first of the robots. Del stuck his tongue out at the big man's receding back, immediately regretting it as Rwm'dek stifled a giggle.

He turned to the girl. 'Why do you put up with him? Do you not just want to… punch him in the nose or something?'

Rwm'dek shrugged. 'He's the best in his field.'

'He's a bully.'

'I can handle him.'

'You shouldn't have to handle him, you should just…' Del sighed. 'I dunno what you should do.'

Rwm'dek squeezed his arm and flashed him a dazzling smile. 'You're very sweet, but I'm not a helpless little girl. If you really want to take my mind off Keely, stop being so shy and ask me if I'd like to go to that new café on the harbour.'

Del's mouth dropped open in surprise. The Flisk girl shrugged. 'I've been waiting five days for you to ask me. Unless of course you don't want…'

'No, no, no,' Del shook his head. 'I do.'

'Good.' Rwm'dek smiled at him again. 'It's a date then. Now I'd better get on with these confirmation checks. Catch you in a bit.'

'Right. Yes. Bye.' Del watched as she hurried over to the nearest robots, Keely starting his constant barrage of chastisement as she drew near. A broad smile spread out over the young museum curator's face. This trip was turning out to be better than he could have possibly imagined.

He turned back to the ice wall, trying to dismiss thoughts of Rwm'dek's deep brown eyes and to concentrate on the task in hand. He hoped that he'd actually put some half-decent clothes in his suitcase as well as his work gear and equipment.

With new purpose, he swung the digital camera from his shoulder. Keely might not want him to touch anything, but he couldn't stop him taking some photographs. It was vital that the excavation of the paintings was documented at every stage. There was no knowing how the pigments would react once they were exposed to the air.

He gave a cry of pain as he caught hold of the metal casing of the slim camera, almost dropping it. Stupid. He'd not put his glove back on and the cold metal had taken the skin from his palm. He shook his hand. Keely had been right. Taking his glove off had been daft. Everything was so cold down here that he'd been lucky not to tear a great chunk of flesh off.

Cursing his stupidity, Del stooped down to pick up his discarded glove. He snatched it up of the floor and frowned.

It was wet.

He stooped down again, shining the light from his helmet across the floor. The floor was sodden, rivulets of water trickling towards the centre of the tunnel. Del shook his head. It was impossible. Everything should be frozen down here.

The rivulets had become a small river now, and slush was starting to pool around his feet. He could feel something too, a tremor that seemed to be coming from *inside* the ice itself. Del nearly called for help then stopped himself. There was probably a perfectly simple explanation and he had no desire to make himself look any more stupid than Keely already thought he was.

He placed his gloved hand lightly on the ice wall. There *was* a vibration from inside the ice, and something else… Del bent forward to get a closer look. There. Back in the depths. A dark shadow, distorted out of all recognition by metre upon metre of frozen water. It was big. How had they missed it before? Del struggled to make out the shape, leaning until his nose was almost touching the ice wall. The silhouette didn't seem human. Were those legs he could see? Four, no six…

The thing in the ice moved.

Del tumbled backwards landing painfully on his backside, sending boxes crashing from the anti-grav sled. He could hear Keely bellow from the darkness.

'What the devil is going on? I thought I told you not to touch anything.'

Before Del could reply, there was a deafening crack and the ice in front of him fractured from floor to ceiling. Slush poured from the fissure, Del cried out in shock as the icy water sluiced over his legs.

He felt strong hands grasp the hood of his jacket, hauling him to his feet. He was spun round, Keely catching hold of his collar, the light from his torch right in Del's face. The big man stared in disbelief at the gaping hole in the ice. There was a low rumble, and a huge chunk of ice crashed to the floor from the tunnel ceiling. Rwm'dek appeared at his shoulder, her eyes wide. 'What did you do?'

'We'll worry about what he did later,' snapped Keely. 'Reposition those robots before the entire place comes down on us.'

Del waved frantically at the crack, trying to force out the words past his chattering teeth. 'In the ice… s-s-something…'

'What are you jabbering about?' snarled Keely. 'There's nothing—'

Like striking cobras, two thin, black arms whiplashed

out of the hole in the collapsing ice. Long fingers wound around the construction manager's grizzled skull and, with a snap, he was dragged into the fissure, his body bouncing across the floor like a rag doll.

Del McAllen and Rwm'dek stared at each other in stunned silence for what seemed like an eternity. Then there was a horrifying scream from somewhere deep in the ice.

'Run,' said Del.

Eyes full of fear, the Flisk girl turned to run, but there was another terrifying crack and a huge section of the tunnel wall collapsed. Del could see something huge and fast moving through the chaos.

'Rwm'dek!' Del screamed her name. He could see those thin, sinuous arms snaking down the tunnel, fingers grasping. Trying to block out the terrified screams Del scrabbled desperately over the blocks of ice towards her. He crashed against something hard and metal: one of the robots. Rwm'dek was clinging onto one of its legs, kicking at the fingers that wound around her leg. With a bellow of anger, Del threw himself forwards, snatching up a pickaxe from the floor and swinging it with all his might at the snake-like arms.

The axe chopped into flesh and muscle and there was an unearthly shriek of pain. The arms snatched back, and Del scrambled over to where Rwm'dek lay gasping.

'Are you all right?'

She nodded, ducking as more ice crashed around them. 'But this entire place is coming down.' Del looked up at the robot towering above them. It had a '12' stencilled in bright red letters across its chest. He could hear servos deep in its torso whining under the strain of trying to support the tunnel ceiling. It turned a blank metal face towards them and spoke:

'+STRESSES BEYOND ENGINEERING TOLERANCES. REQUEST INSTRUCTIONS.+'

Del could hear something skittering over the rubble behind them. Claws scraping across ice. He turned and saw the long grasping fingers of the unseen creature feeling their way across the floor towards them.

He looked desperately for any way out. Even as he watched, another section of the tunnel collapsed, burying three of the robots. He stared at Rwm'dek in despair. The Flisk caught hold of his hand. 'It's too late.'

Del shook his head. 'No, we'll find a way.'

'It's too late,' she repeated.

The claws of the creature were close now. He could see the fear in the girl's eyes. Del nodded weakly. 'Do it.'

Rwm'dek leaned back, shouting up at the robot. 'Project compromised. You are to ignore previous instructions and abandon your post.'

'+FAILURE TO COMPLY WITH INSTRUCTIONS WILL RESULT IN LOSS OF INTEGRITY OF TUNNEL.+'

The scrabbling claws were getting closer.

'Just do it!' screamed Rwm'dek.

'+UNABLE TO COMPLY. INSTRUCTION WILL RESULT IN INJURY OR DEATH TO HUMAN WORKFORCE.+'

'We're already dead you stupid machine.' Del started to laugh. 'We're already dead.'

He kicked out at the long, black fingers that had started

to clasp at his boot. There was a hiss of triumph from the creature.

'Emergency override code Delta two zero!' screamed Rwm'dek.

'+UNDERSTOOD. ABANDONING POST.+'

Del clasped Rwm'dek's hands and stared deep into her eyes, feeling the warm touch of her mind in his as the robots released the ceiling and the tunnel collapsed.

Out in the endless corridors of the Vortex, the police-box shell of the TARDIS spun and twisted, blown on the time winds like a ship at sea. Inside, in the organic jumble of the impossibly large central console room, Martha Jones threw back her head and laughed out loud as the Doctor emerged from an interior door clutching a large inflatable banana.

'Oh, very elegant.'

'What?' The Doctor looked at her indignantly. Instead of his usual pinstripe suit and long, brown overcoat, he was in large baggy shorts, Hawaiian shirt and sombrero. He pulled on a huge pair of sunglasses and threw his arms wide. 'Perfect for a beach holiday, don't you think?'

'Absolutely. Elton John would be proud of you!'

'I got these from him I think.' The Doctor pulled off the sunglasses and peered at them with a frown. 'Either him or the Mogadeesh of Replanak. Always get those two mixed up.' He tossed the glasses onto the central console and thrust the banana at Martha. 'Now then.' He cracked his fingers. 'Where to go? Where to go?'

Martha wedged the inflatable behind the console room

chair and joined him at the controls. She was dressed in a long, light dress and sandals, quite a change from her usual jeans and leather jacket. The Doctor had promised a break from their adventuring, a day or two away from danger and excitement. A chance to recharge their batteries.

The Doctor seemed more excited about it than she did. He'd been unearthing all sorts of stuff from cupboards deep in the TARDIS; deck chairs, Lilos, even a bucket and spade.

He twisted a control, peering at a readout. 'Sun, Sea and Sugary Shiplanos, that's what's in order.'

'Sugary what?'

'You've never had a Sugary Shiplano? Aw, you haven't lived! It's like a liquid candy floss, but it's lighter than air, so it floats and you have to hold onto the straw that you drink it through to stop it floating away.'

Martha shook her head. 'I never know if you're winding me up or not.'

'It's true! Were all the rage in 2050, bloke in Weston-super-Mare found the recipe in the wreck of an Androgum space hopper that crashed in the Bristol Channel.'

'So that's where we're going is it?' Martha folded her arms. 'All the beaches in time and space, and you're gonna take us to Weston-super-Mare?'

'Course not.' The Doctor grinned at her, darting around the console prodding at switches, twisting dials. 'I know a lovely little place, nice beach, good hotel, nice restaurants…'

The glass column in the centre of the control room started to glow with power, and hidden engines started to groan and grind. The entire room was shuddering. Martha gripped the edge of the console. She always loved this, the moment just before they stepped out into somewhere new.

There was a loud thump, and the TARDIS gave a lurch.

'OK.' Martha's eyes were shining. 'Where are we?'

The Doctor snatched his sunglasses off the console, grabbed her by the hand and dragged her towards the door. 'Saudi Arabia. Late twenty-first century. Best Beach of the Century in *Bartholomew's Planetary Gazetteer and Time Traveller's Guide.*'

He hauled open the door, and Martha gave a yelp of surprise as the blast of icy wind hit them. The Doctor stared in disbelief at the snow and ice that stretched out ahead of them.

'Sun, sea and Sugary Shiplanos?' gasped Martha, glaring at him and desperately trying to rub some warmth back into her bare arms.

The Doctor gave a big sigh and wiped the snow from his sunglasses. 'Don't suppose you'd fancy a frozen Shiplano instead?'

ONE

The Doctor locked the door of the TARDIS, thrust the key deep into his jacket pocket and wandered over to where Martha was waiting for him. He was now in his usual suit and coat, and Martha had changed into clothes more suitable for an arctic environment – heavy ski pants and a thick parka.

The Doctor's earlier exuberance had given way to puzzlement. He had checked the readings on the console and everything appeared to be normal, no anomalies or temporal distortions.

'So, have you worked out where we are yet?' Martha asked, shivering.

'Right where we should be.' The Doctor squinted through the glaring snow. 'Persian Gulf, just down the coast from Dubai.' He nodded through the swirling snow. 'World's tallest hotel should be that way. The Rose Tower.'

'It would be called that,' Martha muttered under her breath.

The Doctor shot her a quizzical glance.

Martha just smiled sweetly at him. 'So how come we've ended up in a blizzard then?'

'Dunno.' He set off across the snow, coat tails flapping.

Martha hurried after him. 'Hang on a minute, where are we heading off to then? Bit daft heading off with the visibility like this. Can't we just hop back into the TARDIS and try again?'

'Gotta find out what's gone wrong first. Can't just go shooting off into time and space without checking where we are, can we?'

He set off though the driving snow, seemingly oblivious to the cold and biting wind.

Martha groaned and pulled up the hood of her parka, all chances of a relaxing beach holiday getting further behind every minute. She struggled after the retreating figure, her boots sinking deep into the snow. It was madness. Despite the Doctor's assurances, Martha was sure that the Persian Gulf was the *last* place on Earth that they were. In fact, there was a fair chance that they weren't on Earth at all.

She struggled up a steep incline. The Doctor was standing at the top, peering through the worsening storm. Her feet skidded on the icy rock and she caught hold of the Doctor's arm.

He nodded through the snow. 'There's something over there. A cliff of some kind.'

'Cliffs. Great.' Martha could see nothing but greyness through the swirl of white. 'Perhaps we can do some rock climbing instead of sunbathing.'

'Exactly.' The Doctor grinned at her. 'Come on.'

Keeping a firm grip on his arm Martha followed him over to what seemed like a sheer cliff face, caked in snow and ice. Ridiculously sheer in fact. Martha craned her neck back. 'It goes up for ever.'

The Doctor was frowning. 'Yes. It does seem that way.' He reached out and touched the surface. 'Too smooth to be natural.'

'Man-made?'

'Dunno.' The Doctor rubbed at the surface with his sleeve. 'Hang on… I can see something. Through the ice.'

He fumbled in the pocket of his coat and pulled out a stubby cylinder of metal. His sonic screwdriver. He made a few adjustments and held it out in front of him, pushing Martha behind him.

'Just in case.'

There was a flare of blue light and a high-pitched whine as the sonic vibrations cracked and crazed the ice surface. Frozen shards tumbled into the snow and a warm, glowing light started to pierce the gloom.

The Doctor bent down and rubbed at the patch he had cleared with his hand. He stepped back abruptly, a startled expression on his face.

Martha caught her breath. 'What is it?'

The Doctor gestured towards the hole. 'See for yourself.'

Hunkering down Martha peered into the light. She stared at the face looking back at her. A young woman. A young woman in a bikini.

With a laugh, the woman waved and ran off. Martha could see along a vast expanse of golden sand, heaving with holidaymakers. The sky overhead was a brilliant blue, the sea alive with the sails of yachts. Martha tapped at the cliff with her knuckles. It was glass. She looked up at the Doctor in disbelief. 'It's a dome. We're inside a huge glass dome. On the beach.'

'Hah!' The Doctor hauled her to her feet and twirled her round in the snow. 'How could you ever have doubted me!'

Ahmed Jaffa slumped down into the chair in his borrowed office in SnowGlobe 6 and stared out of the window. Outside, nestled on its artificial island in the crystal-clear waters of the Persian Gulf, the slim graceful curve of the Burj Al-Arab Hotel arced gracefully into the brilliant blue sky. Further along the beach, surrounded by gently curving date palms, SnowGlobe 7 shone in the glare of the afternoon sun.

He wished he was out there in the sun, instead of being trapped inside with problems and no answers.

Jaffa tapped the screen of the computer terminal, bringing it out of sleep mode. He read the email for the hundredth time: a request for urgent medical assistance. His hand hovered over the 'send' button, unsure what he should do.

He rubbed a hand across his face wearily. World resources were being stretched by the tornado season sweeping through northern Europe; a mysterious viral outbreak in the playground of the rich and famous was hardly going to be a priority. He had watched the news footage this morning of St Paul's Cathedral, its dome torn apart by a class-three tornado that had swept through central London. The human race was being torn apart by the very planet that they were trying to save.

Jaffa grunted. Too little too late. They were paying the price now for lack of action a hundred years earlier.

The buzzer on the desk shattered the quiet.

He stabbed at the button impatiently. 'Yes?'

'Dr Jaffa.' It was Marisha, the senior nurse.

'Yes, Marisha, what is it?'

'Director Cowley is here.'

Ahmed groaned inwardly. 'All right, send her in.'

He sighed and leaned back in his chair. The Director would want answers, and he wasn't sure he had any answers to give her.

The door to the office swung open with a soft hiss and Beth Cowley entered. She was a tall woman, with long, black hair cascading down the back of her crisp, dark suit. Elegant designer glasses perched on the end of her nose. It had always baffled Jaffa that she had never sought to pursue laser surgery or use contact lenses to correct her short sightedness.

He rose to greet her, hurriedly minimising the email in his drafts folder. 'Director, I'm sorry. I meant to get over to see you as soon…'

Cowley shook her head and smiled a thin smile. 'No need to apologise, Ahmed. I'm aware of how busy you must be.' She gestured for the sweating doctor to sit back down. 'Please.'

Jaffa sat back down.

The Director sat in the chair opposite him, hands

resting neatly on her crossed legs. 'Now, have we made any progress?'

Jaffa licked his lips, knowing that Cowley wanted results.

'My team are working on the egg sacs, but we've still had no success in matching them to any known creature, living or dead. Really, we're at much the same place as we were. Those in the medical bay are stable, the new cases that we admitted yesterday are the last ones reported. So far at any rate.' He leaned forward across the desk. 'For God's sake, Beth, we need to get a full medical team in here. I'm a medical officer for a small facility, I can't handle something of this scale. We could put in an emergency request to the World Medical Council. Get a quarantine of the area—'

'No.'

'But we've still not established cause.'

'I will not ask for the imposition of a quarantine that will cripple hundreds of businesses.' Cowley's voice was sharp. 'Not until you provide concrete evidence that our situation here poses a danger to the outside world.'

'Until you've signed your deal with that shark O'Keefe you mean.'

Cowley frowned. 'Discourtesy doesn't suit you, Dr Jaffa.'

Jaffa licked his lips, already regretting his words. 'I'm sorry, Director. It's just…'

'You don't like O'Keefe, and you don't like that I have agreed to deal with him.' Cowley's tone softened. 'I like it even less that you, Ahmed. But the economics of our situation are fairly straightforward. Either we accept O'Keefe's offer, or we lose everything. So, if we can keep this little mishap under control until I have secured our future…' The woman flashed him a dazzling smile. 'Well?'

Jaffa nodded.

'Good. I knew you could be reasonable.'

'But you've got to listen to me. If I even begin to suspect that this could spread…'

Cowley's smile didn't waver. 'Of course, Dr Jaffa.' She rose from her chair. 'Now, I have to meet O'Keefe.'

Smoothing down her jacket, Cowley crossed to the door which slid open with a soft sigh. She paused in the doorway.

'Cheer up, Ahmed. Look at it this way. At least you're a senior doctor in charge of a major facility now… Enjoy it while it lasts.'

The door slid shut, and Jaffa slumped back in the chair. He held his head in his hands. He had an unknown viral infection to deal with, too few senior staff, and a boss who seemed to think that the entire occurrence was no more that a mild inconvenience. What the hell was he going to do?

Marisha El-Sayed watched as SnowGlobe 7's Director of Operations glided out of the office and crossed to the lift. She didn't even give the nurse a second glance.

Marisha didn't like the tall Englishwoman. No. It wasn't that she didn't like her, it was that she didn't *trust* her. She glanced over at the office where Dr Jaffa had taken up residence. The young doctor was out of his depth and he knew it. She turned her gaze to the isolation ward. Their senior consultant, Dr Abdul Al-Bakri, had been amongst the first to be struck down. Six of the senior medical personnel shortly afterwards.

She flushed with anger. Why hadn't Jaffa called for help? It was glaringly obvious that this wasn't the minor viral contagion that he thought. She rose from her seat, summoning up the courage to confront the obviously floundering doctor when a buzzer sounded from the ward. One of her patients needed assistance.

Snatching up her mask, Marisha hurried into the isolation ward.

Martha stumbled in the snow for what seemed like the millionth time, cursing under her breath.

'You OK?' The Doctor looked back at her.

'Oh yeah. Just great. Having a whale of a time!'

'Fabulous!' The Doctor grinned, seemingly oblivious to her sarcasm, and set off through the blizzard again.

They had been following the curve of the wall for nearly fifteen minutes now. The Doctor had surmised that if they were in a man-made structure – designed to keep the cold in and the heat out – there would have to be an airlock of some kind. All they had to do was follow the edge of the dome until they found it. Martha had pointed out that the curve of the dome was so gradual that it could be nearly five or six kilometres in circumference, and they had no idea which direction this supposed airlock might be. The Doctor had merely set off in an anticlockwise direction saying that he had 'a hunch', and she'd had no choice but to follow in his footsteps.

Man-made or not, the weather inside the dome was decidedly unruly, and the snowstorm continued to batter at them. Keeping a wary eye on the Doctor's receding form, Martha stopped to shake the snow from her hood. The Doctor was acting as if it was a gentle walk on a summer's day. How that whippet-thin body was staying warm she had no idea.

She was about to set off after him when a dark shape flickered across the edge of her vision. Martha stopped, peering through the swirling snowflakes. Had she imagined it?

No. There. The shape was motionless amongst the brilliant white, no more than a blur in the distance. She strained to see. There was a noise barely audible above the wind, a harsh, cricket-like chirruping.

'Doctor,' she called out, not taking her eyes from the shadow in the snow.

There was no reply.

'Doctor?'

Martha turned to where he had been. With a sudden panic she realised that she couldn't see him any more. She glanced back at where the shadowy shape had been.

It had gone.

Slowly she started to move, wading through the knee-deep snow, following the trail left by the Doctor. Way off to her left, something darted past her, circling ahead. Gasping, Martha tried to move faster, the snow fighting her at every step. There was a burst of harsh clicking from somewhere behind her and, to her horror, Martha realised that there was another shape stalking her through the blizzard. The clicking from behind her was answered by more from her right. Whatever these things were, there were three of them!

Martha threw herself forward, snow stinging her eyes. She no longer tried to keep track of the shapes around her, her only thought was to get to the Doctor.

His trail in the snow was getting more and more indistinct. With horror, she realised that the worsening storm was starting to cover his tracks. Her heart was pounding with the effort of moving through the snowdrifts. 'Doctor!' she yelled, gasping for breath. 'Where are you?'

She stopped, breathless, hands resting on her knees, trying to summon up reserves of energy. A barrage of chittering echoed off the huge vertical expanse of the dome wall. With a cry of fear, Martha forced herself on.

And a dark shadow loomed up in front of her.

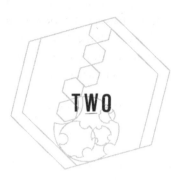

TWO

Martha lashed out blindly, and her fist connected with something hard. There was a cry of pain.

'Ow! Watch it. That hurt!'

Martha felt relief wash over her.

'Thank God! I thought I'd lost you.'

'Well I could hardly go far, could I, we're in a dome, remember?' The Doctor rubbed at his arm. 'That's gonna bruise, you know. You don't know your own strength, Martha Jones.'

'Doctor, there's something in here with us.'

The Doctor stopped rubbing his arm and fixed her with a searching stare. 'Something? What sort of something?'

'Well, I don't know, do I?' Martha gestured into the glaring whiteness. 'I saw a shape. Three shapes. Small, fast. There was a noise…'

On cue, a barrage of clicking and chirruping erupted in the distance.

'A noise like that by any chance?' The Doctor head was

cocked on one side, listening intently. 'Interesting.' He closed his eyes, holding his head back, straining to catch sounds above the wind. 'They're using echo-location, like whales or dolphins.'

Martha clutched at his arm as dark shapes flitted about in the distance.

'Ow!' The Doctor winced. 'Watch my bruise.'

'Doctor, they're getting closer.'

'Yes they are. I wonder *what* they are.'

There was more clicking and the shapes came closer.

'Hungry?'

'Quite possibly.'

'You don't suppose it's like a zoo, do you? You know. Wildlife park at a holiday resort?'

'And I've landed us in the equivalent of the bear pit?' The Doctor grinned at her. 'Not a bad deduction, Miss Jones!'

'Thanks, but can you save the flattery for *after* we get out of here?'

'Yes, you're probably right.' The Doctor rummaged in his pocket and pulled out his sonic screwdriver again. 'If they're communicating by sonar and echo-location, then I should be able to make things a little bit uncomfortable for them.' He held the slim tube out in front of him. 'Cover your ears.'

Martha clamped her mitten-clad hands to the sides of her head. The Doctor pressed a button, and there was a blaze of electric blue light and piercing whistle. Even through her gloves, the noise set Martha's teeth on edge: it was like a dozen nails being drawn slowly down a blackboard.

The effect on the unseen creatures was immediate.

Their clicking became high-pitched and agitated and, with a flurry of snow, the dark shapes vanished.

The Doctor nodded with satisfaction and caught hold of Martha's hand.

'Right. That's seen to that lot for the moment, but let's not hang around.'

Holding the sonic screwdriver out ahead of him like a torch, the Doctor hauled Martha through the snow. From behind them, the clicks and ticks of the creatures settled back into their regular pattern. They were being stalked once more.

Beth Cowley stepped from the lift into the atrium of the main administration building of SnowGlobe 6. Two receptionists sat behind a huge, curving desk of polished teak, and near the doors a bored-looking security officer stared out of the wall-length window.

Beth crossed to the doors, heels clicking on the marble floor. The security guard straightened as she approached, not quite snapping to attention, but acknowledging Beth's authority. She liked that. It was more respect than she got from her own administrative staff.

She had taken over the administration of SnowGlobe 6 less than four months ago. The previous Director of Operations had made a number of stupid errors of judgement, and at one time there had been fears that the environmental damage to the ice might be irreversible. The SnowGlobe Initiative had insisted that, even though SnowGlobe 6 was primarily a leisure facility, the administrative control should rest with someone with the requisite scientific knowledge to ensure that the ice sheet was protected.

Beth gave a deep sigh. If she had realised just how much work the leisure facility required, and just how much it would disrupt her own precious projects at SnowGlobe 7, she might never have agreed to take over. But then, if she had never taken over the running of SnowGlobe 6, she'd never have met Maxwell O'Keefe...

Huge glass doors slid open with a soft hiss, and Beth stepped out onto the decked veranda, her glasses darkening, adjusting to the glare. From below her came the babble of excited voices, the clink of china and the swish of skis on snow.

Beth leant on the railing for a moment. SnowGlobe 6 *was* beautiful. The vast glass dome gleamed above her, the sun blazing through thousands of crystal-clear panes. Thin polycarbide struts criss-crossed the blue of the sky, vanishing into the haze where wispy clouds wreathed the distant mountain peak. Behind her, the administration building swept up in elegant tiers, following the curve of the glass, arcing round to link up with the hotels and chalets that clung to the circumference of the dome.

Below her, steps led down to a wide promenade dotted with cafés, bars and restaurants. The more expensive establishments hugged the dome wall, offering their clientele a choice of views: snow-capped mountain on one side; sun-drenched sea and palm-dotted beaches on the other.

O'Keefe had already chosen one of those restaurants for their meeting. She could see him – an inelegant lump of a man in an ill-fitting suit – perched at a table on one of the balconies. He was a man with expensive tastes, but then SnowGlobe 6 was not a place to come if you were trying to holiday on a budget.

Beth felt wave of anger wash over her. She was about to hand her life's work to a billionaire playboy, a shallow, worthless waster who had had wealth and celebrity thrust into his hands without the slightest effort on his part. Beth clenched her fists. It was so unfair.

She took a deep breath, composing herself. Unfair or not it was the only choice that they had left. Without Maxwell O'Keefe – or to be more precise without Maxwell O'Keefe's *money* – then SnowGlobe 7 was finished. And that meant that *she* was finished, and she had worked too hard to let it all end now. All she had to do was to keep their little incident under wraps for a few hours longer.

Ku'ra Debrekseny rubbed his aching back and glanced over to where his manager was peering intently at a large mechanical digger, inspecting the machine with military precision, copious notes being scribbled into the small, flat PDA that constantly hung around his neck.

Ku'ra groaned, There was no question as to who would be typing up those notes when they got back to the hotel later. He straightened, wincing as his back cracked alarmingly.

'Hey, Brian,' he called across to where his colleague was photographing pieces of mining equipment laid out in neat rows on the concrete floor. 'What do you say we get ourselves a couple of hours on the slopes this evening?'

Brian Williams lifted his head and shook it solemnly. 'I'm not sure when you think we're going to get any time for that sort of thing. Mr Harrison has got a very busy schedule for us.' He turned back to his work.

Ku'ra gave a deep sigh. That much was certain. Mr Harrison had had a very busy schedule for them from the moment that they had boarded their plane. He hadn't been able to believe his luck when this assignment had come up. Dubai. Sun-soaked beaches, crystal-clear oceans. Plus the added bonus of one of the world's best indoor winter sports facilities.

Ku'ra stared around the dark, echoing, empty entrance hall of SnowGlobe 7. This was not quite what he had in mind.

Ku'ra, Brian and Harrison were part of the investigative team sent out by the insurance company to assess the damage caused by the tragic construction accident of a few days ago. They were by no means the largest company of their kind, nor the best known, but so many of the larger companies were embroiled in the constant stream of devastation being wrought across Europe by the ever-worsening climate.

Ku'ra had actually been watching the newscast about the accident when his phone had rung. It had been Laurence Harrison telling him to get a bag packed and to be ready to meet him at the airport in the morning.

On the plane, Harrison had proudly told them that they were to prepare reports for the British Museum in London and for Maxwell O'Keefe. Ku'ra still couldn't work out why a vacuous sponger like O'Keefe would have anything to do with a conservation project like the SnowGlobe Initiative, but a trip abroad was a trip abroad.

He'd been stuck in underground tunnels or in the darkened, disused rooms of SnowGlobe 7 ever since. The only glimpse he'd had of the sun or the opulent majesty of SnowGlobe 6 was from the bus to and from here every morning and evening.

Ku'ra sighed and turned back to his work. They'd been going two days and so far it seemed fairly straightforward. A tunnel collapse, most probable cause at this stage a defective construction robot. There had been three casualties: two human males and a Flisk girl. They still hadn't found the bodies under the rubble. Ku'ra felt a pang of sadness. There were too few of his kind on this planet to lose one to such a stupid accident.

He shook his head. He was being selfish. All three deaths were senseless, not just the death of one of his own kind. He picked up one of the rock fragments that had, in its way, been responsible for bringing about that accident. At first glance it was just a nondescript piece of stone, its surface faintly grooved. It was only when you looked closer that you realised that the grooves were ordered, not random, and the hand of man suddenly became apparent in its design.

Ku'ra couldn't understand what all the fuss was about, but the team from the British Museum had been adamant that these scrawlings from the ancient past were important and Mr Harrison had been equally adamant that they would all be fully catalogued.

Ku'ra placed the stone fragment back in its tray. He was

reaching for another memory stick for his digital camera when a metallic clang made him start.

From across the deserted expanse of the foyer of the SnowGlobe facility, a warning light had started to flash next to the airlock door. Ku'ra frowned. The place was meant to be deserted, the only people inside were the three of them and the security team. He put down his camera on the abandoned ticket desk and made his way over to the huge steel shutters. There was another clank and the whine of motors starting up.

'What on earth do you think that you are doing, Mr Debrekseny?'

The low, melodious voice in his ear made Ku'ra jump.

'Mr Harrison.' He turned and saw the accusing face of his employer peering at him.

'I thought I asked you to make a full inventory of the archaeological specimens, not go wandering off and causing a fuss, hm?' The broad Welsh accent echoed off the metallic doors. Harrison frowned as more metallic clangs rang through the cavernous space. 'Have you been touching things that you shouldn't?'

Ku'ra shook his head. 'I was by the counter when I heard something. Came to see what it was.'

'Sounds like someone inside the dome, Mr Harrison.' Brian Williams had joined them, peering up at the huge doors.

'Nonsense, Brian. Don't be so daft. Who's going to be inside the dome now, eh?'

A klaxon started to blare and a metallic voice grated from hidden speakers.

'PLEASE STAND CLEAR. AIRLOCK DOORS OPENING.'

With a deep, throbbing hum, the doors began to move. The three men backed away.

Laurence Harrison adjusted his tie nervously. 'Brian, would you be so kind as to alert the security guards at the entrance that we may have intruders, please.'

Brian Williams didn't wait to be asked twice. With a backwards glance at the door, he vanished at speed across the dark foyer, footsteps ringing out through the gloom.

Ku'ra tensed. In the gap between the doors, something was moving.

Harrison gave a shrill cry as two figures burst into the foyer in a flurry of snowflakes.

One of the figures, a man, darted across to the door controls, his hands dancing across the buttons in a blur. The other figure, a woman, slumped to her knees, gasping for breath.

The klaxon sounded again.

'PLEASE STAND CLEAR. AIRLOCK DOORS CLOSING.'

With a resounding clang, the doors slammed shut. There was a few moments of almost deafening quiet, then the man let out a delighted whoop of triumph.

'Oh yes! Well done, Martha Jones. If they award medals for escaping from unseen arctic predators, then you just got the gold.'

The woman struggled to her feet. 'The next time you decide to take me on a holiday, can we just settle on Spain, or the south of France. Somewhere simple!'

The man bounded over to her and gave her a quick hug, then stopped, noticing Ku'ra and Harrison for the first time.

'Oh. Er, hello. Sorry, didn't see you there.'

Ku'ra shot a look at his manager, waiting for him to say something. Harrison was watching the two strangers in open-mouthed disbelief. He shook his head as if trying to prove to himself that it wasn't some bad dream, then flushed a deep purple with indignation.

'What the devil do you think you are doing, sir? Don't you realise that you are trespassing in a restricted area?'

The man gave an embarrassed shrug. 'Are we? Terribly sorry. Got ourselves a bit lost. Well, I say a bit lost, *actually* we're exactly where I thought we'd be, only...' He tailed off, peering around the gloom, his nose wrinkled in puzzlement. 'Where *is* here exactly?'

'It's a zoo isn't it?' The woman pulled down the hood of her parka. 'We're in a zoo of some kind?'

'A zoo?' Harrison spluttered. 'You are in SnowGlobe 7, as you must certainly know!'

'SnowGlobe. Right. Lovely.' The man looked around at the deserted foyer. 'Off-season are we?'

'Sir!' The word practically exploded out of Harrison. 'Would you kindly tell me who on earth you are and what you are doing here!'

The new arrivals looked at each other for a moment, then the man started rummaging in his jacket. 'Just a mo. Got some papers here somewhere. I'm the Doctor, this is Miss Jones...'

'Doctor?' exclaimed Harrison.

'Yeees.' The man stopped his frantic rummaging. 'Doctor.'

'Well why the devil didn't you say so? I was hoping they'd sent for you days ago.'

A look of surprise crossed the man's face. 'So... You've been expecting me?'

'Of course we have!' Harrison stepped forward and shook the man firmly by the hand. 'Laurence Harrison. From Harrison, Wheedle and Kr'eekst, loss adjusters. Delighted to meet you, Doctor!'

THREE

Martha had to hand it to him, the Doctor knew how to keep his cool, even when he was totally out of his depth. Despite his obvious surprise, he had swiftly managed to take complete control of the situation, ingratiating himself with Harrison and managing to divert him from asking any uncomfortable questions as to how they had managed to get inside the dome in the first place.

'Been telling those idiots to get you over here from the day we arrived,' Harrison blustered. 'Let me introduce you to my team. This is Mr Debrekseny.'

A tall, man with a delicate, blue-green tint to his skin gave the Doctor a nod, then turned to Martha with a dazzling smile. 'Martha, was it?'

She nodded. 'That's right.'

'I'm Ku'ra.' He shook her hand. His skin was cool and incredibly soft. He gestured to the steel doors. 'What were you doing inside the dome?'

Martha felt her heart sink. It had been going so well.

'Oh, well, you know… Thought we'd get in early.' She struggled to shrug out of her parka. 'Check things out whilst it was quiet.'

A frown crossed Ku'ra's face. He obviously wasn't buying it.

'Why didn't you come to the administration block first? Surely you'd have contacted the Director?'

Martha was getting worried. This was beginning to sound like an interrogation, and she wasn't sure quite what she should be saying. She decided to brazen it out. 'The Doctor and I thought it would be best if we made our own initial examinations before contacting anyone. Form our own conclusions.'

Ku'ra nodded thoughtfully, his eyes narrowing.

Martha held the young man's gaze, pleased with herself. That had sounded convincing enough. There was suddenly a slight tickle at the back of her mind. She shook her head.

The Doctor was suddenly at her side, helping her with her jacket. 'You're a Flisk aren't you?' he smiled thinly at the blue-skinned young man. 'Not a Flisk name, is it, Debrekseny?'

'Er, no.' Ku'ra looked flustered. 'Flisk mother, Polish father.'

'Interesting. Does the Polish side influence your telepathic ability at all?'

Ku'ra flushed a deep sea-green and looked away. The Doctor shot Martha a warning glance. That had been for her benefit. The tickle in her head had been Ku'ra. She felt herself getting angry. How dare he!

The sudden awkward silence was broken by the sound of booted feet ringing through the dark. A short, breathless man accompanied by three security guards in neat, light uniforms, crossed to Mr Harrison. The guards eyed the Doctor and Martha suspiciously.

The Doctor rolled his eyes at Martha. 'I get the feeling that the psychic paper might be working overtime in a minute,' he whispered. 'Let's just hope it works with Flisk.'

Beth Cowley sipped at her coffee and tried to keep herself calm. Maxwell O'Keefe seemed oblivious to her discomfort, telling her his grand plans for the revitalisation of SnowGlobe 7 between huge mouthfuls of omelette.

Beth had tried to impress upon him the importance of the conservation side of the SnowGlobe project, how they should be looking at keeping as much of the ice sheet as possible as untouched as they could, but O'Keefe had dismissed her with a contemptuous wave of his hand.

'People are bored with conservation. The only way that they're going to keep giving you money is if they're going to get some fun out of it. Look at this.' He had gestured expansively at the people around him. 'Every one of these lovely people is paying more than you earn in a month just to be here; meanwhile you struggle with funding, just because you can't agree to loosen up a little.' Ignoring her protests, O'Keefe had started to talk about ski slopes, ice hockey, even a toboggan run between the two domes.

Now Beth took a deep breath and shuffled the papers on the table in front of her. It was all that she could do to stop herself screaming. 'But you do agree that there should be a commitment to continuing the scientific research that we are doing here?'

'Sure.' Bits of egg tumbled down O'Keefe's expansive belly. 'I'm a great fan of science, always have been.'

'So you will agree to sign the contract in its current form.'

O'Keefe gave her a humourless smile. 'Let me finish my breakfast, darling, then we can talk about the exact terms of your contract here.' He winked at her and went back to demolishing his omelette.

Beth raised her coffee cup to her lips, restraining herself from throwing its contents all over the brutish oaf in front of her.

Her phone suddenly rang. She jumped, spilling coffee over her shirt. Cursing under her breath, she pulled the phone from her jacket. The number displayed was Jaffa.

'This had better be important, Ahmed.'

'I think you'd better come outside.' The doctor sounded panicked.

'I'm a bit busy, at the moment,' she hissed.

'A doctor has arrived… Two doctors.'

'What? I warned you Jaffa…'

'I swear it's nothing to do with me, but I just had a call from security. Mr Harrison reported an intruder in SnowGlobe 7, and it seems it's a doctor and his assistant.'

'I'll be right there.' She snapped the phone shut, her heart pounding.

O'Keefe looked at her, with amusement in his eyes. 'Problems, Director Cowley?'

'A small matter that requires my attention, nothing

more.' She stood, dabbing at the coffee stain on her shirt with a napkin. 'Would you excuse me for a few minutes?'

O'Keefe grinned at her. 'I'm in no rush, Director. You take all the time you need. I'll just finish my breakfast and then have a leisurely look at the terms of your contract.' He pulled a red pen from his jacket. 'Perhaps make a few little adjustments here and there.'

Forcing a smile to her lips, Cowley turned and left the restaurant, hurrying towards her office.

Dr Jaffa was waiting for her on the veranda, pacing nervously. She resisted the urge to pick him up by the collar and shake him till his teeth rattled.

'What the hell do you think you are doing, Jaffa?' she growled. 'I warned you…'

'I didn't do anything. I've no idea where they came from.'

Aware that their raised voices were attracting unwanted attention, Cowley caught the quivering medical officer by the arm and led him away from the veranda.

'Get over to my office. Stall them.'

Jaffa shook himself loose. 'Don't be stupid, Beth. It's over, we can't cover this up any more. We should tell them everything.'

Cowley shook her head, feeling panic rising. 'We're so close, Jaffa. O'Keefe is reading through the contract now. If he finds out—'

'But this Doctor, he can help! With luck, we can contain the outbreak now, stop it in its tracks.'

Cowley nodded. Perhaps Jaffa was right. The problem wasn't keeping the infection secret from everyone, just from O'Keefe. And only for the next few hours. 'All right, Jaffa. You head over to the office. I'll stall O'Keefe and meet you there.'

Dr Jaffa nodded.

'And Jaffa. Impress upon them the need for discretion. If this falls apart now then it's as bad for you as it is for me.'

Jaffa scurried away through the crowds. Cowley took a deep breath. So close. She was so close…

Martha stared out through the windows of the coach as it crept its way along the beachfront. The beach itself was beautiful, a picture-postcard combination of clear blue water, pale white sand and gently swaying date palms.

Every few metres, driveways peeled off from the road, snaking out along whitewashed jetties to needle-thin hotels perched on artificial islands, their rooftops peppered with helicopter pads and shuttle bays. It was a playground, albeit a very expensive one.

Martha grinned. 'I hope you've got a robust credit card, Doctor,' she murmured.

Ahead of her, rising from the sand like a vast jewel, was another of the glass domes, similar to the one that they had just left. Mr Harrison had insisted that he accompany them to SnowGlobe 6 so that he could introduce them to Director Cowley.

The Doctor seemed quite relaxed about things, but Martha had a feeling in her bones that, despite the idyllic surroundings, he'd managed to land them in trouble again.

She tugged at the neck of her thermal vest. She felt

uncomfortable, despite the air conditioning of the coach. What had been perfectly fine for the sub-zero temperatures was now horribly inappropriate. She desperately hoped that they'd be able to get back to the TARDIS at some point to change.

She reached inside her parka jacket and pulled out a crumpled brochure that she'd picked up from the deserted foyer of SnowGlobe 7. 'The SnowGlobe Initiative – a Bold Conservation Project for a Changing World,' proclaimed the cover. Martha started to flick through it, her curiosity turning to shock as she started to grasp the realities of a world that was only a few scant years ahead of her own.

By the middle of the twenty-first century, global warming had changed the climate dramatically. Extreme weather was now commonplace throughout the northern hemisphere, and Martha looked in disbelief at the photographs of destruction wrought by tornadoes in cities like Paris, Rome and London.

With temperatures rising and the ice sheets in both the Arctic and the Antarctic looking increasingly likely to be lost for ever, the governments of the world had made a concerted effort to preserve what little they could. Twelve huge domes – the SnowGlobes – were constructed at key cities throughout the world. Then vast areas of ice were literally scooped up from both the Arctic and the Antarctic and set down in their new locations, preserved from the ever-rising temperatures on the planet.

At first, the domes had been a purely scientific endeavour, a noble attempt to keep a threatened ecosystem safe for future generations but, as time went on, the cost of maintaining the domes had begun to become both an economic and political issue.

Reluctantly, the SnowGlobe Initiative had agreed to accept funding from private businesses, and those businesses had their own ways of ensuring that the domes made money. Winter sports, an industry that had almost been wiped out, was now the latest craze sweeping through the rich and famous. Of the twelve domes, only three were still purely scientific establishments: SnowGlobe 3 in the Australian Outback, SnowGlobe 9 in Japan and SnowGlobe 7 here in Dubai. The rest were ski resorts, winter retreats, exclusive hideaways for film stars and politicians. The planet's greatest conservation project had become a thriving entertainment industry.

Martha closed the brochure, unsure of whether to be appalled at how such a noble endeavour had been subverted or happy that, against all odds, a unique environment had been preserved.

She stared out at the happy holidaymakers scattered across the beach, wondering just what the rest of the planet that she called her home must be like in this future that was so terrifyingly close.

The Doctor glanced over to where Martha sat transfixed by the view. He smiled. A holiday in a place like this was just what they needed to recharge their batteries. He craned his neck to look back at the impressive glass dome that they had just left, his smile fading. Unfortunately they had landed in the middle of something that might well interrupt that holiday. As usual.

The Doctor gave a deep sigh. 'It never rains…'

'Doctor?'

The Doctor turned. The young Flisk, Ku'ra, slid into the seat next to him, a sheepish look on his face. The Doctor said nothing.

'I just wanted to say… sorry.'

The Doctor fixed him with a piercing stare. 'I don't think it's me that you should be apologising to.'

Ku'ra was practically squirming in his seat. 'No, it's both of you I've offended. I've tried approaching Miss Jones, but she can be a little…'

'Intimidating?'

Ku'ra gave a nervous smile. 'Yes.'

The Doctor's tone softened. 'Keep at it. If I know Martha Jones, she'll probably accept that apology, eventually.'

'I hope so.'

'She might make you work for it though.'

Ku'ra took a deep breath. 'Thank you.'

'Are there many Flisk in Dubai?' The Doctor leaned back in his seat. 'I would have thought it was a little hot here for a damp-loving race like yourselves. Hardly the M'treeki lakes.'

Ku'ra stared at him in surprise. 'You know about my home world?'

The Doctor gave a thin smile. 'I was onboard the medical frigate *Talaha* when the rift opened during the crossing of the Opius Expanse.'

Ku'ra's jaw nearly fell open. 'You were with the Flisk armada? But that was nearly forty years ago, you can't have been more than…'

'Oh, I was a different man back then.' The Doctor ignored Ku'ra's puzzled expression and let his memory drift. 'You would have liked Flissta. An entire planet of lakes and hills.'

'My mother showed me pictures…'

The Doctor shook himself from his reverie. 'You should spend some time in the Lake District. Closest thing they have on Earth to where you come from.'

Ku'ra nodded. 'A lot of my people settled there. I keep meaning to go.'

'Which brings me back to what brings you to Dubai.'

Ku'ra nodded to where his boss, Mr Harrison, was seated. 'The accident.'

'Yes, the accident.' The Doctor stroked his chin. 'What can you tell me about that?'

Ku'ra shrugged. 'I'm not sure I can tell you much more than you must already know.'

'Tell me anyway. It's always good to get a different perspective.'

'Sure.' If Ku'ra still had any suspicions about the Doctor and Martha, these were pushed aside by his desire to make amends for his earlier indiscretion. He explained how SnowGlobe 7 was in the process of being converted from a purely scientific establishment to a leisure facility, similar to SnowGlobe 6, and how that work had been interrupted by the discovery of prehistoric artefacts that must have been scooped up when this particular section of the Arctic had been excavated.

The Doctor leaned forward, intrigued. 'What sort of artefacts?'

'Carvings, mostly. Pictures on pieces of rock. That discovery caused uproar of course. The entire scientific community up in arms, pointing out that this sort of discovery was precisely the sort of thing that the globes were set up to protect.'

'How come they had only just been discovered?'

'They were widening one of the access tunnels. They're planning a toboggan run between the two globes.'

The Doctor gave a wry smile. 'So the discovery was made by the very people that the scientific community are objecting to.'

'They had an expert over from the British Museum to do a survey when the tunnel collapsed.'

'Anyone hurt?'

Ku'ra nodded. 'Three people were killed. The museum guy and two engineers. They've still not found the bodies.'

The Doctor pursed his lips thoughtfully. 'But they managed to find the rock paintings.'

'And a couple of construction robots. Then they closed the tunnel down.'

'Closed it down, why?'

'The first team to arrive after the accident ended up in hospital. Infection is the rumour. They're not telling us much.' Ku'ra frowned. 'That's why you're here, surely?'

'Yes. Of course. Thanks, you've been really helpful.'

'Mr Debrekseny, could I trouble you for a moment?' Harrison's rich voice rang through the coach.

Ku'ra groaned. 'Sounds like I'm needed.'

'No rest for the wicked.'

Ku'ra slid out of his seat. 'If you'd tell Martha…'

The Doctor smiled. 'I'll put in a good word for you.'

'Thanks.'

The Doctor watched the young Flisk make his way through the coach to where his employer was waiting for him. Through the windscreen ahead of them, SnowGlobe 6 gleamed in the sun. The Doctor narrowed his eyes. Mysterious creatures, ancient artefacts and a strange infection. 'I'd be very surprised if those three things aren't linked somehow,' he murmured to himself.

He looked up as Martha sat down next to him.

'Been chatting with our telepathic friend, have you?' She glared at him.

'Our somewhat sheepish telepathic friend. You might want to give him a second chance.'

'Yeah, well, we'll see. So what's the deal here?'

'I'm not sure yet. There's a lot of unknowns.'

'Why does that not surprise me!' Martha groaned. 'Do I get the idea that our relaxing holiday is becoming a more and more remote possibility?'

The Doctor just smiled at her.

FOUR

Deep in the snow and ice of SnowGlobe 7, the thing stirred fitfully in the ice. Around it, the mews and cries of its three offspring echoed though the biting wind. The prey had eluded them and they were getting hungry. The warm-blooded things that it had sensed had all gone now, but it could feel the minds of so many more outside the walls, out in the heat and the glare.

Claws scraped on rock. The huge black bulk quivered and the creature gathered last reserves of energy. It had been dormant in the ice too long, slept for millennia. Now it needed to build its strength. To do that it needed to feed.

Brian Williams gave a deep sigh and settled back down to get at the work in hand. It was typical of Ku'ra to jump ship as soon as there was some distraction or other.

The two of them had been working together for the last three months. It wasn't that Brian didn't like the young Flisk, but Ku'ra just didn't seem suited to the job, his mind always wandering, always on the lookout for some diversion.

Brian, on the other hand, was happy to concentrate on the tasks that he had been given. The work that they were doing out here in Dubai was an important break for the company. Mr Harrison was convinced that it could be the beginnings of something big for Harrison, Wheedle and Kr'eekst. Brian was determined that he was going to be right there at the forefront when the break came.

He scanned down the list on his laptop. If he could get the assessment of all unaccounted excavation equipment completed by the time Mr Harrison returned…

He looked over to where the three security guards were still loitering on the far side of the darkened foyer, chattering animatedly in Arabic. One of them shot a withering glance in his direction. Brian flushed. The guards hadn't been too pleased to discover that the 'emergency situation' he had insisted was taking place was just a false alarm. They were even less pleased to be told that they were to wait in the foyer and be of assistance to Brian whilst Mr Harrison and the others were over at SnowGlobe 6.

Brian took another deep breath. If he needed their help, then they would just have to do as he said. Mr Harrison had delegated responsibility, and Brian was going to take that responsibility seriously.

He stood up, smoothing down the creases in his shirt, and crossed to where the security team – two tall men and an even taller woman – were leaning against the reception desk. They went quiet as he approached, eyeing him suspiciously. Brian cleared his throat.

'I was wondering if you could help me with some of the machinery that was brought up from the tunnels?'

One of the men rolled his eyes and the woman muttered something under her breath. Brian mentally kicked himself at his choice of words. *I was wondering if you could help me.* Not exactly showing that he was in charge there, was he? These were soldiers. They understood orders. He glanced at the nametags sewn onto the breast pockets of their lightweight uniforms. The men were privates, Kassim and Balsora; the woman, Farrah, was their commanding officer.

He pulled himself up to his full five foot six. 'Right now, if you don't mind, Captain Farrah.'

Farrah straightened, towering over Brian, glaring down at him. Brian held her gaze, suddenly and unexpectedly transported back to his childhood, to the myriad encounters with the gangs of girls that always seemed to rule the playground of his old-style comprehensive school. He could see the smiles on the faces of the woman's colleagues, recalling similar smiles on the faces of bullies all through his life.

The noise cut through the foyer with shocking suddenness. A crash of metal ringing out through the foyer like the clash of a huge cymbal.

The security guards' entire demeanour changed in an instant. Rifles were unshouldered with frightening speed, needle-thin lines of scarlet light from laser sights slashing through the darkness.

The noise came again and again. A metallic booming, deafeningly loud. Brian stared, his mouth agape, as the huge airlock doors to the SnowGlobe quivered under impact after impact. Farrah caught Brian by the arm, pulling him behind her protectively, one eye pressed to the sight of her rifle. With a flick of her hand, she gestured to her colleagues. They fanned out across the foyer, balanced on the balls of their feet, guns trained on the huge doors.

One of them scurried to the wall of the dome, rubbing at the glass with a gloved hand, peering into the swirling snow beyond.

'What is it?' hissed Farrah.

Kassim leaned closer to the glass, cupping a hand over his eyes. 'I can't see.'

'All right. Open the door. Slowly, Kassim.'

Kassim tapped a series of commands into the panel on the wall. Klaxons started to blare and, with a grinding of gears, the huge doors started to inch apart. When they were open about half a metre, he hit the emergency stop button and with a clunk the doors stopped moving.

Brian held his breath, eyes fixed on the snow that swirled through the gap. Kassim edged forward, his gun wedged tight against his shoulder, finger hovering over the trigger.

'Anything?' snapped Farrah.

Kassim shook his head. 'I'll try to—'

Two long, black arms whipped out through the gap in the doors, thin, sinewy fingers winding about the soldier's head. With an anguished cry, Kassim was snatched through into the dome, his body bouncing off the metal doors with a sickening crack and vanishing into the swirling snow.

There was a moment of stunned silence. The two remaining security guards stared at each other in disbelief, then darted forward, rifles raised. They had barely made it halfway across the foyer when something large and dark stepped out through the doors.

The coach swung through the elegant airlock of SnowGlobe 6 and pulled up in a sweeping car park just inside the wall of the dome. The doors swung open with a hiss, and the Doctor hopped out into the crisp, cool air.

Martha stepped down beside him, staring at her surroundings in awe. Despite herself, she had to admit that they had done a fantastic job of converting a scientific project into a holiday resort. The centre point of the dome was a vast mountain peak, one side a gentle curve of soft snow and ski slopes, the other a harsh crag of rock. Cable cars criss-crossed the vast interior of the dome and the sun glinted through the delicate tracery of steel trusswork high above them. Hotels and restaurants jostled for space, and everywhere were people in brightly coloured winter coats: climbers, skiers, families. The entire place exuded wealth.

The Doctor took a deep lungful of air. 'Not bad for a primitive bunch of apes.' He flashed a dazzling smile at her. 'You should be proud, against all odds this has been preserved for the future.'

Martha nodded. 'I guess so.'

Behind them, Laurence Harrison struggled off the coach, bulging briefcase in hand. Ku'ra stepped down beside him.

'Right-ho, Doctor,' puffed Harrison. 'We should get on up to the Director's office, get you properly introduced.' He nodded at one of the cable-car stations. 'That's the quickest way, awful lot of stairs otherwise.'

The Doctor nodded thoughtfully. 'Tell you what, Mr Harrison, why doesn't Mr Debrekseny take Martha to meet the Director, whilst you and I take a closer look at these service robots that were found in the tunnel?'

'What?' Harrison looked flustered.

'Surely you've checked on the remains of the robots?'

'Well, a preliminary assessment has been made.'

'Then let's make a follow-up assessment! If the memory banks of these robots can be accessed then perhaps we can get a better idea of what caused the accident.'

'But the Director, the medical officer…'

'Oh, Dr Jones is perfectly capable of assessing the medical implications. I'd far rather get to the heart of the investigation. You and me, Mr Harrison, cutting through the red tape.'

'Well, if you think that it's important, then of course.' Harrison swelled with pride. 'Now, Ku'ra, if you can take care of these.' He handed the briefcase to his bewildered assistant, fumbling with various notes and papers.

Martha crossed angrily to the Doctor's side. 'Thanks a bunch!'

The Doctor caught her by the arm, leading her to one side. 'Look, Martha, I need you. Something's not right here, and there's certainly more going on than Mr Harrison is aware of.'

'You think it's got something to do with those creatures?'

'Well it would be a huge coincidence if it wasn't. Whatever it is, I want to find out sooner rather than later. If we split up, we've got a better chance of finding out what's going on before anyone realises we're not who we say we are. Get up to the medical bay, bully your way in and see what you can find out about an infection that might be connected with the tunnel, I'll get in touch with you later. Besides…' He winked at her. 'It'll give young Ku'ra a chance to apologise to you properly and, who knows, perhaps a holiday romance is just what's in order.'

With a grin he bounded across the car park. 'Come on, Mr Harrison. Let's go and see what we can find out.'

Martha watched him go. 'A holiday romance. Right, Doctor, that's *just* what I was hoping.'

She turned to where Ku'ra was waiting forlornly for her. He gave her a shy smile.

Martha sighed. 'Come on then. Lead on.'

Brian Williams stared in horror at the creature that had stepped from the swirling blizzards of SnowGlobe 7.

It was as if someone had thrown together a strange amalgamation of monkey, spider and bat. It was tall, nearly two metres, its thin body covered in a thin layer of coarse, wiry fur. Eight long, stick-like limbs sprang from a squat torso, thin spidery fingers feeling tentatively at floor and walls. It moved slowly, while a long tail, tipped with barbs, curled and thrashed agitatedly in the air behind it. The head was large and rounded. Brian could see no eyes, but a twisted, fleshy nose sniffed at the air.

Strange clicks and chirrups filled the air, the thing cocking its head this way and that between each burst of noise. Brian could feel vibrations deep in his stomach, like a very low bass note at a rock concert.

The creature turned in his direction, and Brian took an involuntary step backwards, his shoes scraping on the concrete floor. The thing threw its head back and screamed, revealing layer upon layer of sharp, yellowing teeth.

With terrifying speed, it launched itself forward.

Time seemed to slow for Brian, he felt his foot catch on something, could feel himself start to fall backwards, arms pinwheeling frantically as he tried to regain his balance. He could see Farrah dropping into a low crouch, swinging her rifle up to take aim, the red dot from her laser sight startlingly bright on the black fur of the monster. On the other side of the doors, Balsora already had his rifle up, shouting something in Arabic, his own laser beam tracking the creature as it bounded across the foyer.

Brian hit the ground hard as both security guards opened fire.

The noise was terrifying. Brian screamed and rolled himself into a ball as shots ricocheted off stone and metal. Spent bullet casings bounced off the concrete floor like metal raindrops. The creature gave a shriek of pain as bullets tore through flesh, sending it crashing to the floor.

Farrah and Balsora darted forward, firing burst after burst into the thrashing, twisting shape. Long, grasping hands flailed in the air, the creature lashing out at its tormentors. Farrah danced out of the way as the creature slashed at her, the clawed fingers tearing ragged gouges in the floor. She kicked at the flailing arm with her boot, ducking in closer and lining up her laser sight on the creature's head. There was the rattle of machine-gun fire, then silence.

Brian raised his head, looking in terrified disbelief at where the two security guards stood panting over the twisted corpse of the creature.

Farrah prodded at the corpse with the barrel of her gun. She looked up at Balsora nodding grimly.

'It's dead.'

Balsora swore loudly. 'What's dead? What is it?'

Farrah turned towards Brian, her eyes cold. 'You. Do you know anything about this?'

Brian shook his head. 'No. Why should I know anything?'

Farrah crossed to where he lay, dragging him to his feet. 'Because you said that there were strangers in the dome earlier. Did they mention anything about this… this thing?'

'The girl…'

'What about her?'

'She asked if this was a… a zoo of some kind. I thought that it was odd at the time—'

'You thought that it was odd?' Farrah gave a sniff of disgust. 'But you didn't think to mention it?' She jerked a thumb back at where her colleague was examining the sprawled corpse. 'What do you think this is?'

'I don't know, I…'

The words died in Brian's throat. He grasped at Farrah's arm. 'Behind you!'

Farrah turned, colour draining from her face as a harsh metallic clicking rang through the foyer.

Two more of the creatures had emerged from the dome, feeling their way almost delicately with their long black fingers. Alerted by the creatures' staccato sounds, Private Balsora struggled to get a new ammunition clip into his gun.

Brian watched in despair as the old clip clattered to the ground and the creatures' heads snapped towards the noise. Like striking cobras, the pair launched themselves at the unfortunate security guard. Balsora didn't even have time to scream. There was a frenzy of limbs as the monsters engulfed him.

Farrah gripped her rifle, her knuckles whitening.

'Get out of here,' she whispered.

Brian continued to stare at the feeding monsters, unable to move.

'I said get out of here!' Farrah grasped his arm, her nails digging painfully into his flesh. 'Get over to the other dome, tell them what's happening.'

Both the creatures were looking towards them now, their eyeless heads bobbing and weaving, clicking and tapping.

Brian turned and started to run. Behind him he heard the roar of gunfire and the bellowing of the monsters. Ahead of him, sunlight streamed through the windows set into the main doors.

All he had to do was make it through those doors and he would be safe.

Brian made it no more than a few steps.

He felt something sharp and strong grasp him by the ankles, and he crashed painfully to the floor. Winded, he tried to struggle to his feet but a dark shadow loomed over him.

Brian screwed his eyes up tight, not wanting to see the nightmare that he knew was behind him. The sound of gunfire had been replaced with Farrah's screams of pain then, mercifully, Brian could hear no more.

FIVE

The Doctor followed Laurence Harrison down a long, wide service tunnel that snaked around the outer edge of SnowGlobe 6. Little had been done to add frills or niceties to these corridors and passageways, unlike in the rest of the facility: all the style and elegance had been reserved for the paying guests.

Harrison puffed and panted his way down a winding stairwell, trying to impress the Doctor with facts and findings that they had made since arriving in Dubai.

The Doctor felt a brief pang of guilt about deceiving the earnest Welshman, but he needed to find out as much as he could as quickly as he could, and a service robot collected from the scene of this accident seemed like his best bet.

Harrison stopped in front of a set of gleaming metal doors. 'Here we are.' He waved his ID badge across a reader, and the doors slid open with a soft hiss.

The Doctor stepped into a huge, well-equipped workshop. Workbenches lined one wall, piled high with tools and machine parts. Well-maintained machinery dotted the workshop floor and at the back of the room, dominating everything, were the robots.

'Oh, aren't you gorgeous!' The Doctor gave a whistle of admiration and crossed the room to look at them. The robots were a good two metres tall, each one set into an alcove in the workshop wall. Wires and tubes from diagnostic machinery wound around the glittering metal torsos. The Doctor glanced at the numbers stencilled on the chests of each robot. Alcoves 11 to 15 were empty.

'Excuse me, can I help you?'

A broad Yorkshire accent made the Doctor turn. A tall man in an oil-stained boiler suit was crossing the workshop towards him.

Laurence Harrison bustled forward to make the introductions. 'Doctor, this is Robotics Technician Roberts. Mr Roberts, the Doctor, recently arrived to assist us in our enquiries.'

Roberts wiped the oil from his hand with a rag. 'Good to meet you, Doctor.' He shook the Doctor's hand. 'Come to see the remains of our robots?'

'Yes, I was rather hoping that our robotic friends might be able to shed some light on what happened.'

Roberts gave a snort of amusement. 'If you can get anything out of them at all, then you're a better engineer than me. Over here.'

He led the Doctor and Laurence across the workshop to where the remains of several robots were laid out on the floor. 'As you can see, they didn't quite come out of the tunnel intact.'

The Doctor looked in dismay at the twisted wreckage. He crouched down, picking up one of the robot's severed arms. 'This is how they were found?'

'Pretty much.'

'You found them?'

Roberts shook his head. 'That was Ibrahim, Chief Engineer. He and two of the lads.'

The Doctor didn't look up. 'And they're all in the hospital, I guess?'

'Yup.' Roberts squatted down beside him, toying idly with some of the mangled robot parts. 'Still waiting to hear exactly what the trouble is, never tell us nowt down here.'

'And what have you managed to glean from our dead robots, Mr Roberts?' The Doctor fixed him with a steady gaze.

'Not much so far, Doctor. VINTEK System service robots are designed for load-bearing, used a lot in the construction industry, did most of the early construction on our SnowGlobes here.' Roberts poked a finger into a gash in one of the battered torsos. 'Most of this is impact damage from when the roof collapsed.' He paused. 'We did find some odd markings on one of the robots, though.'

'Oh?' The Doctor raised a quizzical eyebrow.

'Been getting the lads to look at it. It's over here.'

The Doctor got to his feet and followed Roberts to one of the workbenches.

The upper half of one of the robots lay partially concealed by a dust sheet. A number '12' was just visible on the scarred torso.

Roberts pulled off the dust sheet, nodding at a set of deep parallel grooves across the robot's metallic skin. 'Don't know what to make of those.'

'Nasty.' The Doctor bent close, pulling a set of thick-rimmed glasses out of his jacket pocket and slipping them onto the end of his nose. 'You've been in the wars haven't you, big fella.' He pulled out his sonic screwdriver, playing the electric blue light across the harsh gashes in the metal.

'Don't suppose you've had any problems with predators recently? Any reports of strange animals?'

'Animals?' Harrison gave him a puzzled look. 'What on earth do you mean? What kind of animals?'

Roberts gave another snort. 'Think that we've got some rogue polar bears or something, do you, Doctor? You've been reading too much in the gutter press. Been wild stories about animals scooped up in the excavations ever since the SnowGlobes started being built.'

'Not polar bears, no. But something scooped up in the excavations, Something in the ice…' The Doctor held Roberts' gaze. 'Is that so fantastic a possibility?'

'Let me get this right.' Harrison's brow furrowed. 'Are you seriously suggesting that these robots were attacked by some kind of creature in the tunnels?'

The Doctor stood up, slipping off his glasses and toying with them idly. 'Those artefacts that were found, anyone manage to put a date on them?'

Harrison shook his head. 'There was some speculation that they were Stone or Bronze Age. That's why Mr McAllen was in the tunnels. To extract the fragments safely and start the process of dating them.'

'Stone Age…' The Doctor chewed on the arm of his glasses. 'So whatever it is has been in the ice for a very long time indeed. Hibernating, suspended, probably woke up hungry…'

'You're serious aren't you?' Roberts was incredulous.

'Oh yes,' said the Doctor. 'It's a perfectly feasible theory. But don't take my word for it, Mr Roberts, let's see if we can get our metal friend here to tell us.' The Doctor tapped the metal torso on the bench.

Roberts shook his head. 'You won't get anything from them, Doctor. I've tried every trick in the book, they're just scrap metal.'

The Doctor held up his sonic screwdriver and grinned. 'Well, I've got a few little tricks of my own. I hope you don't mind if I try?'

Slipping the glasses back onto his nose, the Doctor bent over the workbench and started to unbolt the robot's chest plate.

With an unpleasant smile on his face, Maxwell O'Keefe watched Director Cowley make her way out of the restaurant. It had been obvious that the woman desperately needed to get away from him, and he had taken great pleasure in finding excuse after excuse to stop her.

He mopped up the last remnants of his breakfast with a piece of toast and sat back in his chair, dabbing at his mouth with a crisp white napkin.

He looked round at where a figure loitered at another table and waved him over. The little man scurried to his side, pulling up a seat and looking at him expectantly.

'How did it go, Mr O'Keefe?'

O'Keefe smiled. He liked Rabley. He liked anyone who made him feel important and powerful. Rabley had been his eyes and ears for several years now, a little man with a lot of useful connections and a weakness for expensive trinkets. It hadn't been difficult to ensure that he always worked in O'Keefe's best interests. It had been Rabley who had alerted him to the SnowGlobe Initiative's financial difficulties in the first place.

O'Keefe nodded at the receding figure of the Beth Cowley as she picked her way through the tourists that thronged on the veranda outside the window.

'You were quite right about her, Rabley. Quite desperate to sell, and not too many complaints providing we promise to look after her precious SnowGlobe.'

'So she's going to sell at a good price, Mr O'Keefe?'

'Oh, it's good.' O'Keefe took another look at the contract spread out in front of him on the food-stained tablecloth. 'But not good enough. She's hiding something from us, Rabley. Something that she thinks might change our minds.'

'What sort of thing, Mr O'Keefe?' Rabley looked puzzled. But then Rabley always looked puzzled.

'I don't know yet.' O'Keefe folded up the contract with his hastily scrawled amendments and slipped it into the pocket of his jacket. 'But we shall find out and make a better profit on this deal than you can possibly imagine.'

He looked out through the far window at the crystal slopes of SnowGlobe 7 gleaming in the sunlight further down the beach.

'Is there anyone over there at the moment?'

Rabley followed his gaze. 'A few security guards, and Mr Harrison and his team, of course.'

'Ah yes, our petty little inspector. We'll need to have a word with him before too long, Mr Rabley. Every man has his price, though I can't imagine in the case of Mr Harrison that his price is going to be too exacting, eh?'

Rabley chuckled. O'Keefe liked people who laughed at his jokes.

O'Keefe stood up, brushing crumbs from his jacket. 'I think that we should take a look at our prospective purchase, Mr Rabley, a little tour just to reassure ourselves that Miss Cowley isn't trying to pull a fast one on us.'

Rabley hurried to help with his chair. 'I'll go and get the car, Mr O'Keefe. I'll get them to call the lift for you.' He scurried off, harrying waiters as he went.

O'Keefe gave a satisfied sigh and looked at the dozens of contented, comfortable and wealthy people that milled around him. Soon he would own SnowGlobe 7 and, once he did, he was going to be richer than all of them put together.

Martha stood in the lift watching as the indicator above the door counted steadily upwards.

Ku'ra was standing behind her, and the silence in the lift was starting to get uncomfortable. All the way from the car park, Ku'ra had done his best to be polite and courteous, obviously trying to find the right moment to apologise to her.

Martha hadn't given him a chance. It was mean of her,

she knew, but the Doctor running off and leaving her hadn't exactly put her in the best of moods.

She knew that she should be flattered. He obviously trusted her to go off on her own and glean as much information as she could. It was just that this was meant to be a holiday, time for the two of them to spend some time together on their own without some alien threat or dangerous situation getting in the way. Travelling in the TARDIS rarely offered that kind of option.

With a soft chime, the door of the lift slid open and she stepped out into the corridor. A slight, dark-skinned man hurried forward, grasping her hand, practically gabbling his words.

'Thank God you've come, I was beginning to think we'd have to deal with this all by ourselves. I wanted to call you earlier, but Director Cowley insisted we keep it as an internal affair.' He peered past Martha into the empty lift, completely ignoring Ku'ra. 'It's just you? I'd hoped there would be a team. Dr...?'

'Jones.' Martha extricated her hand. 'Martha Jones. The Doc... My colleague is examining the service robots with Mr Harrison. You are?'

'Ahmed Jaffa. Chief Medical Officer of SnowGlobe 6. Come this way, please.'

Jaffa ushered her along the corridor. Martha couldn't understand why he was in such a blinding hurry.

'What happened to Dr Al-Bakri?' asked Ku'ra.

Jaffa turned, licking his lips. 'You're one of Harrison's men, yes?'

The Flisk nodded.

'He's ill, same as the others. He collapsed in his office early yesterday.'

Ku'ra shot a glance at Martha. 'That's been kept very quiet.'

'A lot of things have been kept very quiet. Now we must hurry, please. If you could wait in the Director's office she'll be along shortly.' Jaffa urged Martha on down the corridor towards the medical facility.

'I'd like to come along,' said Ku'ra.

Jaffa shook his head. 'I'm sorry, that's impossible.'

'I'm sure that Mr Harrison will need to know if anything is going on that might be relevant.'

Jaffa cursed under his breath. 'Very well, but hurry, please.'

The three of them made their way along the plush corridor. At a double set of glass doors, Jaffa stopped, tapping his security code into a keypad on the wall. The first set of doors slid apart silently. Jaffa ushered Martha and Ku'ra inside the airlock, pulling white lab coats off the wall. 'Put these on please.'

As the two shrugged into their coats, Martha shot Ku'ra a dirty look. 'Keeping an eye on me?'

'Seeing if I can be of help. I am trying to apologise to you, remember.'

Martha sighed. The boy was trying his best, and he was right – she could do with some help.

'All right, Ku'ra. Thank you. Apology accepted. Just keep out of my brain, OK?'

Ku'ra flushed, then smiled.

Martha was aware of Jaffa looking at them curiously.

'Is everything all right?'

'Yes, Dr Jaffa. A personal matter, that's all.'

A green light flicked on above the second set of doors and they slid apart. Martha felt air rush past her head into the room. Negative pressure, designed to stop any microbes or bacteria escaping when the doors were opened.

They stepped into a gleaming bright medical bay, neat, ordered and better equipped than any hospital Martha had ever been in. A tall, strikingly beautiful Arab woman in a crisp nurse's uniform looked up from her desk. Jaffa hurried over to her.

'Marisha, this is Dr Jones. She and her colleague have just arrived to offer their assistance.'

Relief flooded over the woman's face. Martha began to feel nervous. Whatever was going on here was obviously terrifying the medical staff. She desperately hoped that the Doctor hadn't dropped her into something that she couldn't handle.

She was wondering how on earth she was going to bluff this one out when Ku'ra clasped at his head and, with a scream of agony, collapsed on the gleaming tiled floor.

SIX

'I don't believe it.' Roberts stared in disbelief as the robot stretched out on his workbench gave a brief electronic burble and swung its newly attached legs onto the floor.

'Come on now, big fella, take your time,' the Doctor encouraged it.

The robot rose unsteadily to its feet and took a few tottering steps across the workshop floor.

'Ha!' The Doctor clapped his hands in delight.

Roberts scratched his head. The Doctor had worked at bewildering speed, building circuitry and mechanisms that the tall Yorkshireman could only guess at. The workbench was awash with discarded components, bits pulled from the Doctor's coat pocket, and countless lengths of coloured wire.

The rest of the technicians had looked on in amazement as the Doctor had practically vanished into the guts of the robot, rewiring, replacing. Deep within the circuitry of the robot's open chest, Roberts could see the dismembered remains of two coffee machines, a control panel for one of the workshop doors and Mr Harrison's electronic notepad.

Everything Roberts knew told him that the lash-up the Doctor had constructed shouldn't have worked. But somehow it did, and he'd managed to achieve in minutes what Roberts and his team had failed to do in days. Roberts was determined that, when this was over, he and the Doctor would sit down over a coffee (once they'd got themselves a new coffee machine) and have a long talk.

With the bulk of the Doctor's unorthodox repairs finished, two of Roberts' team had helped attach the robot's torso to a new set of legs and were now charging up the depleted power cells.

The Doctor snatched up the chest plate from the bench, gave it a quick polish with the sleeve of his shirt and snapped it into place on the towering robot.

'Now then. Let's see what you can remember, hm? Identification?'

There were a series of clicks and whirrs from deep within the robot's metallic skull.

'+IDENTIFICATION. VINTEK CONSTRUCTION ROBOT. SERIES 9. PERSONAL IDENTIFICATION NUMBER TWELVE.+'

'Nice to meet you, Twelve.' The Doctor grinned. 'How are you feeling?'

The robot turned its blank face towards him. '+QUESTION NOT UNDERSTOOD.+'

'Course not. Silly of me.' The Doctor's tone became more serious. 'Perform memory diagnostic.'

There were more whirrs. '+MEMORY SIXTY-EIGHT POINT THREE PER CENT INTACT.+'

Roberts shot the Doctor an admiring glance. 'Not bad.'

The Doctor shrugged. 'Depends if that sixty-eight per cent is the bit we want.' He nodded at the technicians milling around them. 'I'm not sure that an audience is what we need at the moment.'

Roberts nodded. 'Right you lot. Good work. Tea break.'

As the technicians wandered off towards the rest room, the Doctor called to Harrison who was dozing in a corner of the workshop. 'Mr Harrison, you might want to come and listen to this.'

Harrison stretched and crossed where to the Doctor and Roberts stood in the shadow of the patiently waiting robot.

The Doctor took a deep breath. 'Access memory. Relay last given instruction.'

There was a long pause. For a moment the Doctor thought that he had failed, then noise blared from speakers hidden deep within the robot's torso.

'*Emergency override code Delta two zero!*' The voice of a young woman screamed the words, then there was a deafening crash of falling rock, then silence.

Harrison took an involuntary step backwards. 'Good God.'

The Doctor closed his eyes. 'Access memory. Replay previous two minutes.'

There was another pause.

'+MEMORY CORRUPTED. ONLY PARTIAL REPLAY AVAILABLE.+'

The Doctor nodded. 'That's OK.'

The speakers cracked into life again. A man's voice joined that of the girl's, their words indistinct and broken, and in the background the sound of something angry and inhuman, shrieking and hissing.

'… ject compromised… ignore previous inst… ctions and aban… your post.'

'+FAILURE TO … PLY WITH INSTRUCTIONS … LOSS OF INTEGRITY OF TUNNEL.+'

'Just do it!'

'+UNABLE TO COMPLY… WILL RESULT IN INJURY… DEATH TO HUMAN WORKFORCE.+'

'We're already dead you stupid machine! … already dead!'

'Emergency override code Delta two zero!'

'+UNDERSTOOD. ABANDONING POST.+'

The audio stopped, plunging the workshop into silence once more.

The three men looked at each other.

Harrison took a handkerchief from his pocket and wiped the sweat from his forehead. 'What the devil happened?'

'I think it's fairly clear.' Roberts' voice was sombre. 'They deliberately ordered the robots to let the ceiling collapse.'

'But why? Why?' Harrison slumped down into a chair. 'It makes no sense.'

'Oh, I think it makes perfect sense.' The Doctor's face was grim. 'That was the only option left to them. You heard it, didn't you? In the background, the hissing, the snarling. Something was in there with them, and letting the ceiling collapse was a better option than allowing it to get at them. Or letting it get anyone else.'

'This wretched creature of yours?' Harrison was trembling. 'We've just heard three people die, Doctor.'

The Doctor nodded. 'Yes… Three people. And how many more are here in this dome?' He turned back to the robot. 'Access memory. Two minutes prior to previous audio.'

There was another series of rapid clicks.

'+UNABLE TO COMPLY. MEMORY FILES CORRUPT. UNABLE TO COMPLY. UNABLE…+'

'All right, all right, ssssh.' The Doctor patted a metal arm soothingly, then turned and snatched up his jacket off the workbench.

'Mr Harrison. I think that we should find someone in authority and let them know what we've found out.'

Harrison nodded. 'Director Cowley should be informed at once.'

'Good.' The Doctor struggled into his jacket then turned to Roberts. 'Do you think that you could carry on here, see if you can get any more out of Twelve's memory?'

Roberts nodded. 'I'll do my best.'

'Do you also think you could isolate the frequency that the creatures are using for their echo-location?'

'There's a good recording, so it shouldn't be too difficult. I can run it through the isolators that we use to calibrate the sonic lances.'

'Good man.' The Doctor set off towards the workshop door, coat flapping. 'Come on, Mr Harrison, no dawdling.' Harrison hurried after him.

Roberts turned back to the waiting robot and picked up a screwdriver from the bench. 'Right then, let's see what else you've got tucked away in that metal head of yours, shall we?'

Ku'ra was still unconscious, and Martha didn't know whether to scream at him for making her life more complicated or thank him for providing the perfect diversion.

She had only just managed to catch him before he cracked his head on the tiled floor, and she and Jaffa had manhandled him onto a nearby hospital gurney.

Marisha was pulling a hospital blanket over him.

Martha crossed to her. 'How's he doing?'

'He seems OK.' Marisha gave a shy smile. 'I'm afraid that I'm not too familiar with Flisk biology, but he seems fine. Here…'

She handed Martha a slim plastic pad, readouts flickering across a small screen.

Martha panicked for a moment at the unfamiliar piece of equipment, but as she scanned the figures on the little readout she relaxed a little. Pulse, respiration, heartbeat. All were labelled clearly. Most of them seemed normal. Normal for a human at any rate. She remembered what the Doctor had said back in the dome. 'He's only half-Flisk. Apparently his father was human.' She frowned. 'Heart rate seems a little high.'

Marisha nodded. 'That's what I thought. For a moment I was worried that…' She tailed off.

'That what?'

'That he was going to be like the others.' Marisha nodded towards the ward. 'I have a horrible feeling that this is just the beginning.' She shook her head. 'I'm sorry I'm being morbid. You'll want to see the patients, of course.'

'Of course.' Martha hoped her voice sounded more confident than she felt.

'I'll just get you a mask.' The nurse hurried off.

Martha stared through the glass door at the dozen or so patients lying silently in lines of beds in the ward. She prodded idly at the small diagnostic pad. It seemed to be a combined patient's chart, thermometer, stethoscope and personal computer. 'Dr McCoy eat your heart out,' she murmured. 'I could have done with one of these back at medical school.' She pressed a few controls, bringing a variety of different screens up. It seemed relatively simple to operate and was certainly going to help her if she had to bluff her way through this without the Doctor to help out.

'Here you go.' Marisha appeared at her elbow and handed her a small plastic earpiece.

'Thanks.' Martha took it, trying to pretend that it was a perfectly familiar object to her, watching surreptitiously as Marisha slid her own device behind her right ear.

Martha did the same and there was a sudden tingle around her nose and mouth and a slight antiseptic smell caught at the back of her throat. The device was obviously some kind of high-tech sterilised mask. She could see a faint twinkling haze around the nose and mouth of the young nurse.

'Cool.'

Marisha glanced at her. 'I'm sorry?'

'Nothing.' Martha shook her head, reminding herself

that she would have to stop getting excited by things that the people around her took as everyday items.

'I'm sorry if the settings on the steri-masks are a little high, but we really can't afford to take any chances.'

'Of course.'

Marisha swiped her ID card across a panel on the wall. The door swung open softly and the two of them stepped inside the ward.

It immediately struck Martha that, apart from one or two unfamiliar pieces of equipment, the ward could easily have been one of the private wards back at the Royal Hope Hospital. The beds were neat and ordered, pillows and sheets were crisp and white, and all around there was the soft, rhythmic beep of machinery and steady breathing of the twelve men and women that lay in the cool darkness.

Marisha nodded at the nearest patient, an Arab man with a lean, angular face.

'Dr Al-Bakri.'

Martha leant forward to get a closer look. The man's eyes were flickering violently under the lids. Martha shot Marisha a puzzled look.

'Dreams,' the nurse explained. 'It's the same with all of them.'

Martha moved from bed to bed. The faces of all the sleeping patients were the same, each of them in the throes of something that kept their brains and minds tormented even as their bodies slept. Martha studied the little diagnostic pad in her hand, looking for something that might help. There. Encephalographic functions. She slid her thumb over the touch-sensitive controls, and an angular graph line started to etch its way across the screen.

Martha frowned. 'There's a *huge* amount of mental activity! How long have they been like this?'

'Within hours of collapsing.' Marisha sighed. 'It's been getting steadily worse hour by hour. If only Dr Al-Bakri hadn't been affected.'

'Dr Jaffa's here though.'

Marisha rolled her eyes. 'I meant a proper doctor, not a medical officer from a government facility who's probably never had to treat anything more serious than a grazed knee.' Suddenly realising that she might be talking out of turn she shot a glance back at the office. 'That was unfair of me. He's doing his best, it's just that he seems a little…'

'Out of his depth?'

Marisha nodded, her face falling. Martha felt sorry for the young nurse. She gave her arm a squeeze. 'Never mind. The Doctor, *my* Doctor, is the best there is. He'll know what to do.'

'Good. Perhaps he can finally get to the bottom of what these are too.'

Martha followed Marisha's gaze to a long window looking into a large, well-equipped laboratory. On a low examination table were three grey, spherical objects, each sitting in a shallow stainless steel tray. Martha was puzzled.

'Eggs?'

Marisha shrugged. 'As far as we can tell.'

Martha crossed to the window to get a closer look. 'But eggs from what?'

'We don't know yet. It's been driving Dr Jaffa crazy.'

'Can I get a closer look?'

'I'd rather you didn't.' She nodded at the patients. 'So far everyone who has come into direct contact with those things has ended up in here.'

Martha took another look at the egg-like objects. The trays they sat in were filled with a thin layer of grey dust. As she watched, a section of the egg broke away in a shower of particles. 'You think it's the dust don't you? That breathing in the dust has put these people into a catatonic state.'

Marisha nodded. 'Every hour that goes by, they break down further. It's like they're crumbling away before your eyes.'

Martha stared at the eggs, thinking back to the things that had stalked her and the Doctor through the snow and ice of SnowGlobe 7. Three mysterious creatures, three eggs. More than ever Martha wished that the Doctor would hurry up. Marisha, Jaffa and the others desperately needed help, and she was starting to get scared.

Raised voices suddenly shattered the calm, the noise causing several of the patients to moan and twist in their beds. Marisha hurried between them, whispering soothingly. Martha turned angrily towards the door. Outside in the office, Jaffa was arguing heatedly with a tall woman in a business suit. Outraged on behalf of 'her' patients, Martha marched across the ward, pushing open the glass door.

'What the hell do you two think you're playing at!'

Silence fell.

Jaffa cleared his throat. 'Dr Jones, this is the Director—'

'I don't care who you are,' Martha hissed. 'These people are sick and need rest. If the two of you are going to scream your lungs out at each other, you can do it outside!'

For a moment, Martha thought the woman was going to explode. Jaffa visibly cringed as he waited to see what his boss would do. Martha braced herself for the inevitable showdown.

SEVEN

'Is this a private argument or can anyone join in?' A familiar voice drifted across from the doorway, and Martha turned in relief as the Doctor entered the room, Mr Harrison bustling along behind him.

The Doctor caught hold of Jaffa's hand shaking it vigorously. 'Dr Jaffa, I presume. I see you've been introduced to my colleague. Marvellous bedside manner Dr Jones has, don't you think?' He glanced over to where Ku'ra was sleeping on the hospital gurney in the corner of the room. 'Hello, what's been going on here?'

He bent down, lifting up one of the young Flisk's eyelids and examining him curiously.

'Good heavens!' Harrison hurried over to Ku'ra's side. 'What on earth happened?'

The Doctor raised a curious eyebrow at Martha. 'Do I gather that you decided not to accept his apology?'

'Hey!' Martha was indignant. 'I didn't do anything to him.'

'Doctor.' Cowley had regained her composure and was regarding him impatiently.

'Hello? Yes. Sorry. Lots to take in. Miss Cowley, isn't it?'

'Director Cowley.' The woman's tone was icy.

'*Director* Cowley, righto.' The Doctor smiled. 'Sorry. Now then, *Director*, what seems to be the problem here?'

'I wasn't aware that we had a problem, Doctor. And I'm certain that I've not asked for any assistance.'

'Really?' The Doctor peered through into the ward at the sleeping figures. 'Twelve beds full of patients with an unidentifiable disease and you don't think that you've got a problem?'

'A minor contagion that is under control. Dr Jaffa—'

'Dr Jaffa has apparently been asking for additional assistance for some time. Never wise to disagree with your doctor.'

'Jaffa is modest about his abilities.'

'Or perhaps it's just that you're too ignorant to realise the danger that you're putting everyone in.'

Cowley looked as though she had been slapped. 'How dare you!'

'Mr Harrison.' The Doctor's face was grave. 'Perhaps you'd like to tell Director Cowley here what we've just discovered.'

Harrison fumbled with his tie nervously. 'It seems as though there is an animal of some kind that may well have been responsible for the accident.'

'An animal?' Cowley was incredulous.

'Like those things that we saw in the dome?' asked Martha.

The Doctor nodded. 'Seems likely, don't you think?'

'What are the two of you blathering on about!' Cowley was red with anger. 'There are no animals in the dome!'

'Well that's where you're wrong, Director.' The Doctor's voice was like a whiplash. 'Mr Harrison and I have just examined the remains of one of the construction robots that has been recovered from the site of the accident. Its memory banks confirm that just prior to the tunnel collapse the people in there were attacked by one or more predatory animals. Dr Jones and I were also stalked by some kind of animal inside SnowGlobe 7. You have twelve people – including your senior medical personnel – in a comatose condition, and Mr Harrison here tells me that you recovered some egg sacks from the accident site. So shall we stop pretending that there isn't anything going on here and start trusting each other, or shall we just wait until this jolly little holiday camp is knee-deep in bodies?'

All the fight left Cowley's face and she slumped back onto a chair, drained.

Jaffa hovered at her side. 'He's right, Beth. It's gone too far. We need their help.'

Beth Cowley nodded weakly. 'Yes, you're right. Ahmed, would you show the Doctor what data we have collected so far, please.'

Jaffa nodded. 'It will take me a few moments.' He hurried away to his office.

Martha slid over to the Doctor's side. 'So what are these animals, then?' she asked curiously.

The Doctor shrugged. 'Dunno. Not enough information about them yet. Where are these mysterious eggs?'

'In there.' Martha pointed at the laboratory. 'They're disintegrating fast though, turning into some kind of dust.'

'Interesting.' The Doctor rubbed his chin thoughtfully. 'And what about Mr Debrekseny? If you didn't deck him then what happened?'

'Not sure.' Martha looked over to where the young man lay. 'He just went out like a light as soon as he set foot in here.'

'Did he say anything?'

'Nope, just clutched his head and collapsed.'

The Doctor's eyes narrowed. 'Something affecting him on a mental level perhaps.'

'Wouldn't surprise me.' Martha passed him her diagnostic pad. 'All of the patients have got abnormally elevated mental activity.'

The Doctor peered at the readouts, fingers dancing over the controls. 'And with Ku'ra being more receptive to mental stimulation than most humans…' He grinned broadly at her. 'Outstanding work, Dr Jones. I'm beginning to think you don't need me at all.'

'Hardly. When this is all over, you are *really* going to owe me that holiday.'

The Doctor squeezed her arm reassuringly.

There was a groan from the far side of the room. Ku'ra raised his head from his pillow, lifting a hand to shade his eyes from the light.

'Your patient appears to be reviving,' said the Doctor.

The young Flisk was struggling to raise himself up on his elbows.

Martha caught hold of his arm, helping him sit up.

'How are you feeling, my boy?' Harrison was fussing over him like a concerned uncle.

'Groggy.' Ku'ra licked his lips. 'And parched. Got any water?'

'I'll get it.' Marisha hurried over to a water cooler, filled a paper cup and handed it to him.

'Thanks.' Ku'ra drank greedily.

'Hey, slow down. You'll choke yourself.' Martha took the cup from him.

Ku'ra settled back down onto the stretcher. 'What happened?'

'We were rather hoping that you'd be able to tell us that.' The Doctor was watching him intently.

'I'm not sure. I remember coming up in the lift with Marth- Dr Jones. I remember Dr Jaffa meeting us in the corridor and then...' Ku'ra frowned, obviously trying to dredge something up from his subconscious. His eyes widened and he gripped Martha's arm. 'I felt her! Felt her pain!'

'Felt?' The Doctor leaned forward. 'You mean a telepathic contact?'

'Yes. In terrible pain. I wasn't ready for it.' Ku'ra slumped back on the gurney. 'It's something I've always struggled with. Having a human father has meant that I never had the same level of control as my mother did. When a Flisk is near death, there are a lot of... unwanted telepathic contacts. When they are in pain...' Ku'ra looked up at Marisha in anguish. 'You didn't tell us that there were Flisk infected as well. That some of my people were dying.'

Marisha frowned. 'But we don't *have* any Flisk in here. All of our patients are human.'

The Doctor tapped his teeth thoughtfully. 'Are you still getting this mental contact?

Ku'ra half closed his eyes, concentrating. 'It's not as powerful as it was before, but it's still there, yes.'

'Doctor?' Jaffa leaned out through his office door. 'We have that data for you.'

The Doctor patted Ku'ra on the arm. 'You get some rest Ku'ra. Come on, Dr Jones.'

Martha followed the Doctor through into Jaffa's office. It was small and bright, with a long window looking out onto the beachfront. Martha longed to just get out there into the sun. Director Cowley followed them in and sat down on a low leather couch. She seemed to have regained some of her composure. Jaffa beckoned the Doctor over to the desk.

The Doctor dropped down into a chair and pulled himself up to the slim computer, slipping his glasses onto the end of his nose. Data and graphs jostled for position on the screen.

'You've been a busy man, Dr Jaffa.' The Doctor prodded at the keyboard. 'Skin samples, sweat samples, cardiographs, encephalographs…' He peered at the young doctor over the top of his glasses. 'A lot of information telling us absolutely… nothing.'

Jaffa looked uncomfortable. 'We've checked the symptoms against every known disease in the database.'

'So I guess that tells us that it's not a *known* disease. What about these eggs?'

Jaffa leaned over his shoulder and brought up more files of data. 'We've had the automatic systems analysing them ever since they arrived in the laboratory. Under strict quarantine, of course.'

'Of course.' The Doctor's nose was practically touching the screen. 'And everyone who has come into contact with these things has ended up unconscious?'

Jaffa nodded. 'The rescue team, Dr Al-Bakri, half a dozen paramedics and several of the medical staff here.'

'Interesting. And you've had no luck identifying species type?'

Jaffa squirmed again, his gaze flicking between the Doctor and Director Cowley. 'Not so far. Again, we've checked and cross-checked against every animal in the database and are getting no matches.'

'With any *known* species.' The Doctor took off his glasses and leaned back in his chair. 'So we're dealing with a species that is extraterrestrial in origin or one that predates the fossil record, or…' He fixed Jaffa with a piercing stare. 'Did you include human or Flisk DNA in your comparison tests?'

Jaffa shook his head, frowning. 'Of course not. They're eggs. We started with birds and reptiles and expanded our search parameters from there.'

'But Mr Debrekseny is convinced that he had mental contact with a dying Flisk mind…' The Doctor leaned forward, hands dancing over the computer keyboards. 'I love computers, I really do, but they only tell you what you want to hear, and are never very good at just coming up with ideas of their own.' He finished typing with a flourish.

'But you can ask them to run even the most ludicrous ideas through their little metal minds and if there's an answer there then they'll find it.'

Jaffa stared at the screen in horror. 'That's not possible.'

'I'm afraid it is.'

'What is it?' Cowley had got up from the sofa. Jaffa looked over at her, his face white. 'There's a match. The eggs. Flisk and human DNA.'

'But what does that mean?'

'That the "eggs" aren't eggs at all.'

The look on the Doctor's face made Martha go cold.

'Oh, something hatched from them all right,' he went on. 'Several somethings in fact, several somethings that are currently taking up residence in the blizzards of SnowGlobe 7. But the creatures hatched from the remains of your archaeological team. The eggs are the mutated remains of their skulls.'

EIGHT

From inside his air-conditioned limousine, Maxwell O'Keefe watched impatiently as Rabley scampered round the doors of SnowGlobe 7, peering through the glass and shooting puzzled expressions back at his employer.

O'Keefe sighed. The little man was useful, but he wasn't the sharpest knife in the drawer. Curtis Rabley had come to his attention after a failed attempt to rob a wages shuttle at an O'Keefe casino in Las Vegas. The job had gone badly wrong but something about the man's ambition had appealed to O'Keefe. In a strange way, he could see something of himself as a younger man. Oh, his security advisers had all told him that he was a fool, that employing a man who had just attempted to rob them was madness. But O'Keefe had ways and means of buying loyalty, and Rabley had proved himself very loyal indeed.

O'Keefe settled back into the leather seats of the limo and stared out at the huge expanse of empty car park surrounding the SnowGlobe. It summed up the difference between this dome and the other: the spaces here were empty; SnowGlobe 6's were filled with every luxury vehicle known to man. By the time he had finished, this car park would be full to bursting too.

Money had been the driving force behind Maxwell's life. It opened doors and buried secrets, it made him popular and respected. It gave him power. Power over little people like Rabley, power over principled losers like Cowley. He smiled. Taking the dome away from Cowley – watching the effect it was having on her – was very satisfying indeed.

A tapping on the tinted window brought him out of his musings. O'Keefe pressed a stud and the smoky glass slid into the door with a soft whirr. Hot air wafted into the cool of the car's interior, and Rabley's sweat-beaded face peered in through the window.

'Problems, Mr Rabley?' O'Keefe raised an expectant eyebrow. 'Security blathering on about "restricted areas" and "authorised personnel"?'

'That's just it, Mr O'Keefe.' Rabley wiped at his face with a grubby handkerchief. 'There isn't any security. The entire place is wide open.'

O'Keefe tutted. 'Typical of a government operation.'

Rabley shook his head. 'It's not that, Mr O'Keefe. Something's definitely not right. There's no one around at all, and the doors to the SnowGlobe itself look as though they're open.'

'Open?' O'Keefe snorted derisively. 'I doubt that very much. Director Cowley would have their guts for garters if anyone so much as breathed on her precious "protected environment".'

'I'm telling you, Mr O'Keefe, the doors are open. There's snow blowing all over the reception area.'

O'Keefe sighed and hauled himself out of the car onto the baking tarmac. As he'd been saying to himself earlier, Rabley wasn't the brightest of men. Some ventilation system was obviously open, or Harrison's men were conducting some kind of survey. A perfectly obvious explanation, yet Rabley was seemingly unable to sort it out for himself.

'Come along, Mr Rabley. Show me.'

O'Keefe followed the little man across the car park, smiling to himself as Rabley practically tripped over himself as he hurried to open the tall glass doors into SnowGlobe 7's entrance foyer.

He looked around the darkened interior with distaste. Typical of the lack of imagination of a government-run scientific endeavour. Lines of dull ticket booths, a pitifully small shop selling books and trinkets, and an endless procession of informative posters stretching out in a curve around the dome.

Dull, dull, dull. He had never seen the attraction of places like this. He had never liked museums or art galleries. He'd never liked anywhere that purported to be educational. He'd always preferred circuses to zoos, arcades to galleries, shops to exhibitions. All of his own enterprises were bright, audacious and, above all, fun.

Cold air made him shiver. He frowned. Rabley seemed to be right. The airlock doors *did* appear to be open, a line of windswept snow building up on the concrete floor. Strange…

Rabley hovered at his shoulder, skittish and nervous, one hand hovering near the small blunt-nosed pistol that he always had hidden in his jacket.

O'Keefe nodded at the open door. 'See if you can get that closed, Mr Rabley. It wouldn't do for us to buy this dome only to find all of the snow had melted, would it?'

Rabley hesitated, and for a moment O'Keefe actually thought he was going to argue, but the little man obviously thought better of it and hurried over to the door controls on the far side of the foyer.

O'Keefe wandered towards the gift shop. In his mind, he could already see how it would look when he had finished rebuilding, could already see the happy crowds, hear the chink of cash registers.

He stumbled over something in the dark, cursing loudly as he almost overbalanced.

'Are you all right, Mr O'Keefe?'

'Of course I'm all right,' he snapped. 'Just hurry up and get that door closed and then see if you can get some lights on in here before I break my damn neck.'

'Right you are, Mr O'Keefe.'

O'Keefe peered down at the shadows at his feet to try and see what he had tripped over. The floor was sticky. O'Keefe wrinkled his nose in disgust. If he was going to have to bring in specialist cleaning contractors, he would have to have words with Cowley about reducing her sale price still further.

With a series of dull clunks, the lights started to come on all over the foyer.

'I've found the lights, Mr O'Keefe.'

'Thank you, Rabley. That much is obvious.'

The lights had illuminated the thing he had tripped over. It seemed to be a football. A leathery sphere, about thirty centimetres in diameter. He nudged it with his foot. The sphere rolled slightly, dust flaking from its surface. The top was open and cracked. It was more like a giant, half-eaten boiled egg than a football.

O'Keefe lifted his shoes in distaste – a thick goo coated the soles. He looked around for something to wipe his feet on. There. A bundle of rags lurked under the sales counter. He bent to grab them, then stopped in horror. The rags were the remains of a shirt, and inside the shirt were the remains of a body. O'Keefe backed away, staring at the egg. Suddenly there was so much more detail. The remains of what had once been eye sockets, a mouth, wisps of hair.

'Rabley,' he croaked, his mouth dry.

'Nearly got it, Mr O'Keefe. These door controls are a little bit tricky, that's all.'

O'Keefe turned angrily towards his assistant, ready to bawl him out for wittering on about doors when his employer was knee deep in body parts. His anger turned to abject terror as he caught sight of the thing that was sliding silently though the open airlock. O'Keefe backed himself up against a wall as the monstrosity shambled forwards on thin, spindly legs. Amazingly it had walked right past Rabley, who was still hunched over the airlock door controls.

Silently, the creature padded forward. When it reached the centre of the room, it paused, head cocked back, fleshy nose sniffing at the air. Abruptly it let out a stream of high-pitched clicks and whistles that O'Keefe could feel in his gut.

Startled, Rabley spun, hand reaching for the gun in his jacket. His jaw dropped open at sight of the creature, which turned, emitting another stream of noise.

The sound of the gun was deafening. With a screech, the creature skittered backwards, arms flailing wildly. Rabley fired two more shots in quick succession, both of them sending flesh and fur flying from the creature's torso. With a turn of speed that belied his stature, Rabley threw himself towards the main doors, shooting wildly over his shoulder as he ran. O'Keefe held his breath as the creature seemed to gather itself into a ball then hurled itself forward, claws scrabbling on the concrete floor.

At the last moment Rabley threw himself to one side and the creature flew past him, crashing against a stack of crates and boxes, sending them flying. For a moment, O'Keefe thought that Rabley was going to lose his balance amongst the tumbling debris, but, with another volley of gunfire, he regained his momentum and sprinted for the doors.

The creature hissed its displeasure, sending shattered crates flying across the foyer as it clambered back onto its feet. Spitting forth a barrage of clicks it scampered after its prey.

Even though he knew what was coming, O'Keefe couldn't take his eyes from the scene. Rabley was so close, but the creature was so very, very fast. Almost in slow motion, Rabley dived towards the double doors, the sunlight outside tantalisingly close. O'Keefe could see the terror on the man's face as the hammer of his gun clicked uselessly onto an empty chamber. The creature's arms were reaching out for him. Arms, fingers grasping…

As the beams of sunlight from the door touched the creature's flesh, it gave an unearthly, high-pitched, agonised scream and recoiled, writhing on the concrete floor. O'Keefe could swear that he actually saw steam rising from its skin.

Rabley skidded to a halt in the pool of sunlight, unable to believe that he was still in one piece. The door slid silently open, and a waft of warm air swirled though the cool foyer. The creature scrabbled backwards, arms flailing, its cries almost pitiful as it raged against the man that had eluded it.

Rabley stood silhouetted in the doorway, looking helplessly back into the foyer.

'Mr O'Keefe.'

O'Keefe gave a strangled cry, fear and panic rendering him mute. Surely Rabley wasn't going to leave him here alone, not after all these years?

'I'm going to get help, Mr O'Keefe. I'm sorry.'

Rabley vanished into the sunlight and, for a few brief seconds, all that O'Keefe could hear was the pounding of his own heart and the short, sharp breaths of his own ragged breathing. He strained to hear the whimpering of the creature, trying to judge where it was. He was lucky – it still hadn't seen him. The scrabble of claws on metal made him start. The creature had retreated to the relative cool of the open airlock, he could see it squatting in the drifting snow, licking at its wounds. With a jolt of horror, he realised that another of the things was slowly squeezing its bulk though the narrow gap.

In desperation, O'Keefe tried to judge how long the distance was from him to the door. It couldn't be more than fifteen or twenty metres. Could he make it that far before they caught him?

Taking a deep breath, he pushed himself off from the wall, willing himself towards the beckoning sunlight. As soon as he started to move, he knew in his soul that he was never going to make it. Too many years of fine living at the expense of others had given him a physique that was never meant to move at speed. Above the pounding of blood in his ears, O'Keefe could hear the clicks and ticks of the creatures as they gained on him and a low, drawn-out wail that he only realised was his own screaming voice as needle-sharp claws brought him crashing to the floor.

In Dr Ahmed Jaffa's office there had been a few moments of stunned silence and then everyone seemed to be speaking at once. Jaffa kept shaking his head, refusing to believe it, insisting that the Doctor was wrong. Harrison just puffed away saying how preposterous it was. In the end, it had been Marisha who had managed to restore some kind of order, pointing out that they were doctors who were behaving like children and that they had a responsibility to their patients.

Even the Doctor had been cowed by the young woman's forceful bellowing. Martha grinned. She was starting to like Marisha more and more.

The one person who had remained conspicuously quiet

throughout everything had been Beth Cowley. Everything that Martha had been told about her pointed to a forceful, domineering woman, used to having her instructions followed without question. Indeed, the glimpse of her that Martha had got when Cowley first entered the medical bay had reinforced that impression. But now… It was as if the realisation that she was no longer in control had taken all the strength out of her. Martha got the impression that she had been fighting hard for so long, struggling to keep things under her control, that she had given up now everything was starting to unravel, resigning herself to being a spectator as events unfolded without her.

Martha had seen patients in a similar way back at the Royal Hope. The moment when, for whatever reason, they couldn't see the point in carrying on any more and all the fight left them. The Director was just slumped on the sofa, face blank. Martha was getting worried about her. She had tried to talk to the woman, but had got nowhere. She would have to talk to the Doctor, see if he agreed with her.

The Doctor had been working frantically with Jaffa for over twenty minutes now. Once the young medical officer had got over his initial disbelief, he and the Doctor had run the tests again, confirming what the Doctor had suspected. The eggs were indeed the remains of the three initial casualties. They didn't have records for the British man, but they had been able to bring up files for both the construction engineers, and the DNA samples matched.

The Doctor and Jaffa were making a detailed examination of the eggs, the two of them encased in cumbersome bio-hazard suits, looking for all the world like deep-sea divers or spacemen as they lumbered around the cramped confines of the laboratory.

The eggs themselves – the remains of the poor victims of the creatures' attacks – were rapidly disintegrating and, if the Doctor was right, the dust that they created was horrifically contagious. Martha couldn't get over how quickly the transformations must have taken place, the speed with which the alien pathogens had been able to transform three healthy human beings into hosts for these things.

She pulled herself up. Not three human beings – two human beings and one Flisk. Not for the first time, she found her terms of reference to be out of place in the places that she ended up with the Doctor. It wasn't so much a question of learning something new whenever they landed, more that she had to unlearn everything that she took for granted from her old, mundane life.

She looked over to where Ku'ra was sitting sipping at a mug of hot tea. The young man had taken the revelation hard. With so many hardened professionals around, those surrounded by death on a daily basis, Martha had forgotten how it could hit those unfamiliar with it.

She sat down next to him. 'How you doing?'

'OK.' He smiled.

'You sure?'

'Well, not that OK.' He took another sip of his tea, watching the Doctor and Jaffa through the glass of the lab wall. 'What could do that to a person? *Why* would something do that to a person?'

'If the Doctor's right, then these things might not even

have any conscience about it, this might be just the way they survive.'

'And that's meant to make it all right?'

'No, of course not.' Martha squeezed his arm. 'You're worried about Brian and the others, aren't you?'

Ku'ra nodded. 'What is taking Harrison so long?'

Martha glanced at the clock on the wall. Mr Harrison had been the first to remember that there were still people in the dome – Brian and the security team – and had hurried off with strict instructions from the Doctor that they were just to get out of there as fast as possible. Harrison had cautiously pointed out that the security team were heavily armed and they might be able to finish this as quickly as it had begun, but the Doctor had been adamant that they mustn't take any kind of action against the creatures until they knew what they were dealing with. At present, his plan seemed to be containment and study, and to that end he was trying to avoid getting the authorities involved until the last possible moment.

In her heart, Martha knew that any authorities were unlikely to have the Doctor's detachment about the deaths. The creatures might have been unique, unprecedented, but they had proved themselves to be hostile killers.

'Right, we're done in here, is the decontamination suite ready?' The Doctor's voice came over the intercom, words muffled by the bulky suit.

Marisha nodded. 'You first, then Dr Jaffa.'

The Doctor manoeuvred himself clumsily into the small glass booth in the corner of the lab. The door swung shut behind him, and Marisha punched at a set of controls set into a small panel on the wall. A bright white light flooded the booth, the glare making Martha wince. The glare faded, and Marisha consulted a small readout. 'OK, you're clean.'

Marisha pressed another button, and the door on the other side of the booth swung open. The Doctor stepped through, shrugging out of the bulky biohazard suit and bundling it into a locker. He crossed to Martha, his face grim. Martha handed him his coat. 'You find out anything useful?'

'We found out lots. Whether it's useful or not…' He tailed off, looking at the heavy metal case that Dr Jaffa was manhandling into the decontamination booth. 'We've sealed all three skulls into a bio-containment crucible. I'm not sure I can stop the disintegration, but we can at least ensure that the dust that they are creating doesn't infect anyone else.'

'Any idea what sort of creature we're dealing with yet?'

The Doctor chewed his lip in irritation. 'No. Not yet. Whatever it is, its life cycle is *unbelievably* complicated.'

'And it requires humans as hosts?'

'Not just humans. It could just have easily have been rats, mice, birds. It just so happens that the first thing it found when it thawed was humanoid.'

Martha felt a chill. 'So if this spreads…'

'Then we're looking at a pandemic that could spread across every species on the entire planet.'

NINE

Curtis Rabley sat in the driver's seat of Maxwell O'Keefe's vintage 2029 Bentley hybrid, trying to calm his breathing. He cursed as sweat dripped from his brow onto the seat, spotting the tan leather. He pulled his grimy handkerchief from his pocket and dabbed at the damp patch, frowning worriedly. O'Keefe would kill him…

He stopped, a short barking laugh escaping from his lips, and shot a nervous look back at the doors of the SnowGlobe. There was no sign of movement from inside, no sign of the creatures that he had so nearly fallen prey to. Presumably something, or rather some*one*, else had taken their attention.

'Sorry, Mr O'Keefe,' he murmured.

Rabley reached into the glove compartment, pulled out a small box and shook a dozen bullets into the palm of his hand. He wasn't going to take any chances.

Checking that no one could see him, he calmly reloaded his pistol, sliding each bullet into the chamber with methodical precision, giving himself a chance to think, to work out what he was going to do next.

Going back in to try and rescue his employer was a waste of time: it was obvious that he didn't stand a chance. That left him with contacting the authorities. Rabley sniffed with disdain. Even if they believed his story about ravening monsters (and Rabley was still having difficulty believing that himself), going to the authorities would start a long complicated chain of questions about who he was and what his background was – and that would lead to nothing but trouble.

No, his best bet was to contact Mr O'Keefe's office, let them sort it out, though even then Rabley could see that he wasn't going to have an easy ride. O'Keefe's head of security – a South African thug called Bunta – had never exactly been enamoured of him, had tried to stop O'Keefe giving him the job in the first place. What was he going to think when he found out that Rabley had let O'Keefe get himself killed. No, there was no way that Bunta was going to accept that this hadn't been Rabley's fault. There was no way he was going to believe that Rabley hadn't engineered the death himself, and that this wasn't somehow connected with the three million dollars in World Currency that O'Keefe had stashed in the hotel safe.

A bullet slipped from Rabley's hand, clattering into the footwell. The deposit. Three million. His heart was racing. When he had first taken the job with O'Keefe, he had always been on the lookout for an opportunity to defraud the man, to carry out the robbery that he had been intending when he got caught. Gradually, though, he had begun to gain a grudging respect for his employer. O'Keefe had always treated him well, had given him smart clothes and good accommodation, had trusted him in a way that no one had ever trusted Rabley in his entire life. But now...

Rabley stared at the doors to the SnowGlobe. Now O'Keefe was dead, and it had only been the man who had commanded Rabley's loyalty; not the company, not the lackeys and hangers-on, the man.

Rabley snapped the pistol shut, his mind racing. He and O'Keefe had been seen leaving SnowGlobe 6 together, that was certain, and the last person to have spoken to them was Cowley. Sooner or later, someone was bound to figure out that O'Keefe had gone to look over his investment, and the Bentley certainly stood out in the empty car park.

Rabley licked his lips nervously. If he was going to get away with this, everyone would have to believe that he had died at the hands of those creatures, just like his employer. Then he'd need to get back into their hotel unseen, siphon off just enough of the deposit to make the rest of his life comfortable and vanish for ever. Rabley felt a jolt of excitement. This could work!

Carefully, Rabley scrutinised the car park. His first concern was to ensure that he hadn't been seen leaving SnowGlobe 7 and getting back into the car. He needn't have worried: the place was deserted. The only people he could see were too far distant to worry him, and they were more interested in getting to the beach than in some vintage car.

He shook the shells that he had just put into the pistol

into the palm of his hand. He had fired enough shots to ensure that the empty casings would be found easily enough. Now he just needed to convince people that he hadn't escaped.

Throwing the bullets back into the glove compartment, Rabley shrugged off his jacket and bundled it around his gun. With a final look around the car park, he slipped out of the car, locking it behind him and sprinting across the baking tarmac to the big double doors of SnowGlobe 7. He peered through the glass. No sign of the creatures, or of Mr O'Keefe. Tensing himself, he stepped in front of the doors, triggering the sensors. As the doors slid apart, Rabley thought that he could hear a muffled scream and the staccato screeching of the monsters. For a moment, he had a pang of guilt. He shook it from his mind, hurled his bundled jacket with all his might, then turned and fled.

The Doctor and Jaffa were busy transferring the case containing the three mutated skulls into a deep-freeze unit in the hospital morgue. The morgue was small and discreet – presumably because the last thing that people wanted to be reminded of on their holidays was the prospect of death.

Martha watched as they carefully slid the sealed case onto one of the examination tables. Jaffa was still in his bulky bio-suit. Marisha had not been happy about that, keen that he followed established protocols, but Jaffa was tired and stressed and in no mood to play things by the rules.

The sound of booted feet and raised voices outside in

the foyer made Martha start. Mr Harrison had returned, and he wasn't alone: half a dozen stern-looking security guards had arrived with him. The Welshman was sweating and agitated, surrounded by people all asking questions at once. One of the security men – a captain – was speaking animatedly in Arabic with the young nurse.

The Doctor looked up at Martha and raised a quizzical eyebrow. 'Problem?'

She shook her head. 'Mr Harrison is back. With company.'

The Doctor winced. 'Are you happy to finish up here, Dr Jaffa?'

Jaffa nodded. 'I'll get this sealed into one of the vaults.'

'Good man.' The Doctor crossed to Martha, peering at the pandemonium outside. 'What's your professional opinion about Director Cowley, Dr Jones?'

Martha gave him an admiring glance. Despite everything, the Director's slightly odd behaviour hadn't gone unnoticed by the Doctor either.

'I think that too much has happened to her too quickly. She looks like she's well on the way to a total breakdown. Ever since we arrived, it's almost as if she's been sitting back and letting events take their course around her.'

The Doctor nodded. 'Yes, she's on the verge of some kind of collapse. I think that we should keep a careful eye on Miss Cowley, don't you?'

They emerged into the medical bay.

Harrison practically leapt forward. 'Doctor…'

'Mr Harrison. All your team safely out, I hope.'

Harrison shook his head. 'I don't think so. Brian isn't

answering his radio, and they can't raise anyone from the security team.'

'Doctor.' The security captain pushed forward. He was a man in his mid forties, slim with a neat beard, long, dark hair swept back under a peaked cap. A semi-automatic rifle was swung over his shoulder.

The Doctor sighed. This was what he had been hoping to put off for as long as possible, the point when the authorities – presented with something that they didn't understand – responded with guns.

'Yes! Hello!' He turned, smiling broadly. The security guard glared at him.

'I am Captain Hassan. Mr Harrison informs me that you might have some information about… creatures… loose in SnowGlobe 7?'

'Well, yes. That seems as though it might be the case…'

'And Nurse El-Sayed tells me that there is some kind of infection here in SnowGlobe 6 that is connected to these creatures in some way.'

'Yes, also true.' The Doctor scratched at his head. 'What you need to realise is that—'

'What is wrong with you people?' Captain Hassan practically exploded. 'We have almost eight hundred people in this dome, and it is my job to keep them safe. How am I expected to do that duty when the medical team and the Director of Operations herself withhold vital information from me?'

The Doctor's face fell, and, despite herself, Martha had to stifle a laugh. For a moment, he looked like a schoolboy who had been caught doing something he shouldn't.

The silence was broken by a crackle from Hassan's earpiece. He crossed to the window, listening intently, then barked a few words in Arabic and turned back to the Doctor.

'That was one of my security teams. There is no sign of any of our people at SnowGlobe 7. The main doors are unlocked and there is evidence that the integrity of the dome itself has been breached. They also discovered Mr O'Keefe's limousine in the car park. It seems likely that he and his assistant have also gone missing inside the dome. Now if *any* of you can give me *any* information that might be of help before I send my people in—'

'No.' The Doctor's voice was like a gunshot. 'You will not send any more people into that dome.'

Hassan squared up to the Doctor, eyes narrowing. 'Now listen, Doctor…'

'No, you listen to me, Captain Hassan,' snapped the Doctor, all playfulness gone from his voice. 'You listen very carefully!'

Martha held her breath. Suddenly the Doctor seemed to dominate the room. All eyes were on him.

'You don't have the faintest idea of what you are dealing with or how dangerous this situation has become.' The Doctor's voice was low and menacing. 'We are dealing with a creature that is unimaginably old and unimaginably savage. The reason that this dome is not overrun is through luck, pure and simple, and it is only through the swift action of the people in this room that the infection has been halted as quickly as it has. The worst thing that you can possibly do at this moment is to try to deal with this creature as if it was a rabid dog. I have to try and communicate with these creatures, to find out what they are and where they come from. To do that I need time.'

His voice softened slightly. 'Nothing will be served by turning this into a bloodbath. Don't you agree, Captain?'

Hassan tilted his head slightly. 'I want no more deaths, Doctor.'

'Good!' The Doctor clapped his hands. 'That's agreed then. So if you and your men will escort me over to SnowGlobe 7, we'll see if we can sort this out once and for all.'

'Just a minute.' Martha caught hold of his arm. 'You can't just go waltzing off…'

The Doctor looked her full in the face. 'Martha, I've got to. Don't you see. This has gone as far as I can let it go.'

'Then I'm coming with you.'

'No, you are not. I need you here, Martha. I need you to keep an eye on Cowley and help Jaffa and Marisha with the patients here.'

'But you can't go in there on your own.'

The Doctor grinned at her. 'Who said anything about me going in there alone?'

Rabley slipped into the foyer of his hotel, peering over the top of his sunglasses at the concierge, waiting until her back was turned before making his way across to the lift.

As the doors slid closed, he relaxed a little. He'd bought the sunglasses and a revoltingly loud shirt from one of the beachfront stalls, and he became immediately indistinguishable from the hundreds of holidaymakers that thronged the seafront as soon as he slipped them on. No one would give him a second glance now. Besides, O'Keefe always made a song and dance when he arrived back at his suite – insisting that they checked to see if there were any messages for him, making a big fuss about what was or wasn't on the menu for breakfast, generally flirting with any of the girls who were foolish enough to make eye contact with him.

Rabley himself had barely exchanged more than a few words with any of the hotel staff – buried in his employer's ample shadow, no one had given him more than a second glance. That gave him an advantage. With luck, he would be out of the hotel and on his way to the airport within the hour.

There was a ping as the lift arrived on the seventeenth floor. Rabley peered out cautiously into the corridor. Empty. He crossed to his room, swiped his key card in the lock and slipped inside. His room and O'Keefe's were part of a suite on the top floor of SnowGlobe 6's premier hotel. From the huge picture window, the view stretched out down the ski slopes, the roof trusses practically within touching distance.

Rabley pulled a small shoulder bag from his wardrobe, discarding the clothes inside into an untidy heap on the floor then unlocked the connecting door to O'Keefe's rooms. He crossed quickly to the concealed safe and punched in the combination. He pulled the door open and lifted out a large attaché case, placing it on the edge of the vast bed and flicking open the clasps. His heart leapt as he looked at the bundles of crisp notes. He licked his lips nervously. It was so tempting to just try and make off with the entire case. There was more money here than he'd ever need in his life again, but if he did that then O'Keefe's people would *know* that something was wrong. No, for this to work everyone had to believe that he and O'Keefe were both dead.

He pulled a bundle of notes out of the case, flicking them idly through his fingers. He needed to take just enough to make himself comfortable, but not so much that it would arouse suspicion when O'Keefe's people arrived to put things straight. Everyone knew that O'Keefe had expensive tastes, and he'd certainly not been shy of spreading a little of his wealth around over the last few days. There had even been that one night at the SnowGlobe's modest casino. Rabley nodded to himself. Yes, O'Keefe had certainly gone out of his way to get noticed on that occasion, any enquiry was bound to assume that he had spent – and lost – a reasonable amount that evening.

He started to transfer bundles of notes from the attaché case to the holdall. When the bottom of the bag was full, he reluctantly snapped the clasps closed on the attaché case and placed it carefully back in the safe.

He licked his lips. Now was the tricky part. The safe had an internal timer. If he left now, any thorough investigation would show up the fact that the safe had been opened *after* the point that O'Keefe had been killed, and Bunta was bound to be thorough. He had to ensure that the safe records showed that the last time it had been opened was the previous night.

Rabley cracked his fingers. He knew that everyone

thought that he was stupid, that his lack of education made him an ignorant man, but in the field of locks and timers he was a genius.

Allowing himself a brief smile of satisfaction Rabley set to work.

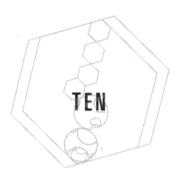

TEN

Technician Roberts looked up in surprise as the Doctor burst into the workshop, followed by half a dozen security guards and Captain Hassan.

Hassan looked around the workshop impatiently.

'We're wasting time, Doctor.'

'Far from it, Captain.' The Doctor beamed up at the towering robot. 'How are you getting on with the big fella's memory, Mr Roberts? Anything more of interest?'

Roberts nodded. 'Fragments, Doctor, nothing more. A few more fractured audio files, some corrupt visual data.'

'Visual data?' asked Hassan. 'You mean you've got pictures of these things?'

Roberts crossed to a small laptop and tapped at the keys. 'Not much I'm afraid. It's had to go through a lot of image enhancement.'

The screen flickered to life, and the Doctor crouched down peering at the grainy image. 'Ooh, nasty.'

The image on the screen was blurred and indistinct.

The Doctor could just make out the shapes of the robots, shovels and oil-drums, and in the background, silhouetted against the white of the ice, the creature.

'What the devil is that?' asked Hassan.

The Doctor slipped his glasses on, tapping the screen and zooming the image. 'I don't know…'

'It's big.'

'Yes. And black. And hairy…' The Doctor slid the image around the screen, trying to get some clearer idea of what sort of creature he was dealing with. It looked part insectoid, part primate. It at least confirmed his suspicions that it wasn't anything from Earth's biology.

There was a whirr of servos and hiss of hydraulics from behind him, and the Doctor looked up in surprise. Service Robot Twelve had taken a step back from the screen.

The Doctor shot a quizzical look at Roberts, and the technician shrugged. 'Some glitch in its processors. It seems to react to any sight of old hairy there.'

'Interesting.' The Doctor scrambled to his feet, patting the robot's arm and cooing softly. 'There, there, it's all right.'

Hassan gave a snort of disbelief. 'Oh, please.'

'Why shouldn't it be frightened?' snapped the Doctor. 'Every generation of artificial intelligence is designed to better mimic its human counterpart. Poor old Twelve here is in the robotic equivalent of shock.'

'So you're hardly being responsible if you're suggesting that you take it back to where it received that shock.' Hassan's voice was laced with contempt.

'Let me be the judge of that. I am the Doctor after all.'

The Doctor looked up at the robot. 'He's the only one who knows what happened down there. He knows where the creature's lair is.'

Roberts crossed to the Doctor's side, rubbing his chin. 'There's still a lot of memory damage. I'm not sure how much use he's going to be to you.'

'Let's find out, shall we?' The Doctor stepped back. 'Service Robot Twelve, do you feel capable of returning to SnowGlobe 7?'

'+FOR WHAT PURPOSE?+'

'To locate the organism responsible for the deaths of your co-workers.'

The robot inclined its head. '+FOR WHAT PURPOSE?+'

'To attempt communication with it.'

The robot stared impassively at him for a moment, hard drives ticking within its metal skull.

'This is pointless,' snapped Hassan. 'We're wasting time here, the thing is defective.'

The Doctor waved his hands at him irritatedly. 'No, no, wait.'

With a whine of servos the robot straightened again. '+THIS UNIT WAS INVOLVED IN THE DEATHS OF CO-WORKERS. THIS UNIT NEEDS TO UNDERSTAND WHY.+'

'The only way we are going to get those answers is if you accompany me back to SnowGlobe 7.' The Doctor cocked his head on one side. 'So what d'you say, Twelve, hm?'

'+ACQUISITION OF ADDITIONAL DATA IS LOGICAL.+'

'Atta boy!' The Doctor snatched off his glasses, slipped them into his pocket then turned and wrapped a conspiratorial arm around Roberts' shoulder. 'How did you get on with that audio data I asked you to process?'

Roberts nodded at a small, squat device on the bench. 'Frequencies isolated and analysed.'

'Fantastic!' The Doctor bent over the machine, reaching for the sonic screwdriver in his pocket. He pressed a stud on the audio analyser and a thin, warbling tone filled the air. He closed his eyes, listening to the tone, flicking a switch on the screwdriver and turning a dial on its side until the trilling from the analyser cut out abruptly.

With a satisfied smile, the Doctor turned to Roberts. 'Now, I don't suppose you'd be able to provide me with any information about the layout of the domes would you? Wiring diagrams, construction blueprints, that sort of thing?'

Roberts nodded. 'I should think so.' He pulled a small diagnostic pad from his overalls. He hooked it up to the laptop, transferring data across with practised sweeps of his hand. The machine gave a series of bleeps then fell silent. Roberts detached it and handed it to the Doctor. 'Everything you should need there, Doctor.'

The Doctor grinned at him. 'Mr Roberts, you are a star.' He slipped the pad into his jacket and rubbed his hands together in satisfaction. 'Right! Come on you lot. No point hanging around down here. We've got work to do. Chop, chop!'

Ignoring the filthy look that Hassan gave him, the Doctor bounded out of the room, whistling at Service

Robot Twelve as if it were some huge metallic dog. The robot lumbered after him.

Roberts watched them go. He got the impression that before long things were going to get an awful lot worse.

In the ice of SnowGlobe 7, the thing stretched its muscles, sharp claws dragging across the frozen walls. Around it, its offspring hissed and snarled, already growing larger and stronger. They had fed well on the warm things that had come into their domain, but they had learned that these warm-blooded creatures could bite, could kill. The bodies of the dead were not wasted though: the bones were picked clean, the flesh reabsorbed.

Its long sleep in the ice had left it weak and vulnerable, but the food it had eaten had renewed it; the young that snarled at its feet had given it purpose. The thing stretched out with its mind. Outside, so many of its prey were gathered, but it could not reach them, not yet. It gathered itself, long arms wrapping around its bulk, straining with sections of its brain long unused. It remembered from long, long ago how the food resisted the call, how it struggled and kicked and screamed.

It reached out with its mind and started to draw in its prey.

In Jaffa's office, Beth Cowley drifted in and out of a troubled sleep. The last few hours had gone by in a blur, and she was just a bystander now, watching helplessly as all her dreams and aspirations slipped slowly away from her. She had convinced Jaffa to give her something to help her sleep, something to dull the headache that had built and built within her skull.

She vaguely recalled someone telling her that Maxwell O'Keefe had almost certainly perished at the hands (the claws?) of the creatures in the dome, but surely that was just a fantasy, a dream. O'Keefe had beaten her, he had won and she had nothing left.

She kept going over and over the events of the last few weeks, always coming back to the same inexorable conclusion. SnowGlobe 7 was finished. Her work was finished. She was finished. She curled herself into a ball on the sofa, willing the pounding in her head to stop. Migraines had always blighted her life. Stress, the doctors had told her, too much time at work and not enough relaxation.

Cowley stifled a laugh. Here she was, in one of the most expensive holiday resorts on the planet, and she was about as far from relaxation as she could get.

She closed her eyes, trying to shut out the babble of voices from outside. A frown flickered across her brow. Above the noise, just on the edge of her perception she could hear something else, a distant voice, insistent and beguiling. A voice that seemed to fill her entire skull. The voice didn't talk to her with words, it spoke to her in pictures, images of the Earth long dead, of distant worlds that she could never have dreamed existed.

Cowley sat up, her head tilted, listening. All her pain and anxiety suddenly left her and there was nothing left but the voice in her head. Suddenly the failure of the dome seemed so unimportant. Why had she ever thought that she would be remembered for something so tiny, so insignificant? O'Keefe had been a fool who had underestimated the power of the creature in the dome and had paid the price for his foolishness.

The voice in her head showed her more and more. The creature had survived millennia in the ice, and now it was here in the dome. Her dome. She was its protector, its saviour! She could hear, feel what it wanted. To feed. To survive. To make the Earth its new home.

Suddenly, she knew what she had to do, she knew what legacy she would leave the world. She rose from the couch, smoothing down her suit, and crossed to Jaffa's desk. The key to the morgue sat in a tray next to his computer.

Snatching up the key, Cowley slipped across the room and peered out into the office. Jaffa and Marisha were in the ward with Martha and the Flisk boy. Harrison was slumped on the bench near the reception desk, too wrapped up in his own guilt to notice her.

She crossed silently to the morgue, unlocking the door and slipping inside. In the cool silence, the voice in her head was stronger. She was calmer than she had ever felt in her life. She hurried to the vault where the eggs had been sealed. She knew now that they were the key to the new world that she would create.

Opening the vault, she reached in and slid out the heavy case, lowering it to the floor, running her hands over the cold metal. Inside was everything she needed to make sure that she would be remembered on this planet for ever.

Resealing the vault, she hefted the case into her arms and crossed back to the morgue door. Marisha had come back into the reception area, fussing over Harrison. Cowley cursed softly. She would have to wait for her moment.

The Land Rover skidded to a halt outside the glittering dome of SnowGlobe 7, tyres squealing on the hot tarmac. Security guards, already jittery about whatever might lie inside the dome, stared in disbelief as a two-metre robot unfolded itself inelegantly from the back of the vehicle, and stomped towards the doors.

The Doctor swung himself out of the car, coat-tails flapping in the breeze that had sprung up from the sea. Completely oblivious to the dozen or so gun barrels that were trained on him, he followed the robot towards the doors. He peered through the glass at the deserted foyer, frowning at the chaos inside. A long, dark stain snaked across the floor towards the open SnowGlobe doors. The Doctor grimaced.

Hassan was barking orders at his men. The Doctor turned to him. 'Have any of your team been inside?'

A dozen heads shook in unison.

'Good. The Doctor reached into his pocket and slipped the sterilisation pod behind his ear.

'You think that the infection could spread?' Hassan asked, his face stern.

'I think that it would be prudent to ensure that no one is exposed unnecessarily, don't you?'

'And if *you* contract the infection?'

The Doctor ignored the question. 'Once I'm inside, I'm going to seal the doors. No one tries to get inside this dome until I say so, is that understood?'

Hassan flashed his perfectly white teeth. 'Absolutely.'

The Doctor turned and patted the waiting service robot on the arm. 'Come on, Twelve. In we go.'

The doors hissed open, and the two of them vanished inside. Hassan watched them go with grim satisfaction, then marched across to the Land Rover and snatched up the radio from the dashboard.

'Get me every man we have. I want both SnowGlobes sealed. No one in or out until I say so.'

From inside the dome, the Doctor watched Hassan, already guessing that the security captain had never intended to simply sit back and wait for him to find out what was going on. He was in a race against time now – he had to make contact with the creatures before the authorities could take control.

He listened carefully for any of the telltale hunting noises of the creatures. Satisfied that they were on their own, he looked up at the robot looming over him.

'How are you with locks, Twelve?'

'+OPERATING PROCEDURES ARE AVAILABLE FOR ALL MECHANISMS IN THE DOME.+'

'Good, 'cos there's a terrible draft in here. Be a good lad and close that airlock door, would you?'

The robot clunked its way over to where the snow was still streaming in across the floor.

The Doctor turned to the main entrance, flicking the switches on his sonic screwdriver and running the electric blue tip of the little device along the rim of the door. Metal blurred and flowed like molten toffee. Outside, the security men, alerted by the glare of the light, pointed and jabbered angrily, pulling uselessly at the now-sealed mechanism and shouting for Captain Hassan.

Satisfied, the Doctor nodded. He needed time, and military 'specialists' clumping around after him would just complicate matters. They wouldn't get the doors open now without blowing them off, and he doubted that even Hassan would be that reckless. Not until he knew what he was up against at any rate.

The Doctor pulled a length of string from his pocket, tied it around the screwdriver and slipped it around his neck. He pressed a stud, and the tip of the sonic device glowed with soft, blue light. Thanks to Roberts' work in isolating the frequencies of the creatures' echo-location, he now had a way of cancelling them out. To the creatures, he was effectively invisible.

He turned to see how his new mechanical companion was doing at the airlock. The big robot was hunched over the control panels, metal hands moving with surprising sensitivity over the controls. The Doctor smiled. The robot was like a huge mechanical child. He would have to help Roberts rebuild its memory before he left.

A sharp clicking noise from inside the SnowGlobe wiped the smile from his face. The robot looked up from its work, its face unable to express emotion but its posture, its entire mechanical body language, gave the impression that it was frightened by the sound. The Doctor launched himself at the doors. Twelve swung its head towards him.

'Don't just stand there, you great metal lummox!' the Doctor bellowed. 'Get those doors closed!'

The clicking got louder. Through the doorway, the Doctor could see dark shapes hurtling towards the airlock door. With agonising slowness, Service Robot Twelve leaned down and tapped in the last few commands on the door access panel.

The airlock doors slammed shut with a deafening clang.

The Doctor skidded to a halt, letting out his pent-up breath in a long sigh.

The robot leaned over him. '+AIRLOCK DOORS CLOSED.+'

From inside the dome, the Doctor could hear the creatures hissing and snarling, their claws skittering on the thick metal of the doors.

He looked at the robot disapprovingly. 'You and I are going to have to have a long chat about cultivating a sense of urgency.'

'Perfect. We'll make a nurse out of you yet!'

Martha nodded in satisfaction at the neat hospital corners on the bed and grinned at Ku'ra. He had made the mistake of offering to help and, after dealing with a ward full of patients on her own for so long, Marisha had jumped at the offer. She and Jaffa were checking on each of the patients in turn, trying a series of tests that the Doctor had suggested, while Martha and Ku'ra followed them around the ward, ensuring each of the patients was comfortable as they moved on.

Ku'ra returned the smile, but the young Flisk had none of the spark that he had had earlier. Martha squeezed his arm. 'Hey. I'm sure that your friend will be all right.'

'Are you?'

'It could just be a faulty radio…' Martha floundered.

'He's dead.' Ku'ra was direct and blunt. 'You know it. I know it. We should never have left him there on his own.'

'But you couldn't possibly have known—'

'No, but *they* did.' Ku'ra shot an angry glance at Jaffa. 'He and the Director knew that something was wrong. You and your friend too. You knew those things were inside the dome, and you said nothing.'

'Hey, we're the ones trying to help, remember,' Martha snapped at him. She reddened, partly out of anger, partly out of guilt that he might be right.

There was an awkward silence for a moment, then Ku'ra shook his head.

'I'm sorry. That was unfair. You're right, no one could have known. It's just Mr Harrison. He's taking this so hard.'

Martha looked out through the glass at where the little insurance man sat forlornly on the bench, head in his hands. He had wanted to try and help find his assistant, but the Doctor had been adamant about going alone. Martha knew that feeling all too well, being left alone when all you wanted was some task to make you feel as though you were doing something useful.

She was wracking her brain for something comforting to say when Ku'ra winced and stumbled. Martha caught him as he swayed unsteadily, pain creasing his features.

'What is it?'

'I'm not sure. Something in my head…'

'Like before?'

Ku'ra shook his head. 'No. It's not another Flisk mind, it's as if…' His eyes widened with surprise at something over Martha's shoulder. She spun to see what he was staring at. In the bed behind her, the patient – a young woman – had sat bolt upright, eyes wide and staring, mouth working spasmodically.

'What the hell?'

Marisha hurried over to her. 'Oh no you don't.' The woman's face curled into a bestial snarl. She lashed out, sending the young nurse crashing to the floor. Jaffa hurried forward, trying to push the woman back down. She tossed him aside with unnatural strength, spitting angrily at him.

'Martha!' called Marisha. 'Tranquilliser pad, on the trolley there!'

Martha snatched up a slim silver device. It didn't look like any tranquilliser she had ever used before. Marisha scrambled to her feet snatching it from her, frantically twisting at controls on the handle.

'I really don't think that tranquillisers are going to be much help.' Ku'ra started to back away.

All across the ward, each and every patient was sitting up, eyes impossibly wide, their posture stiff and unnatural. One by one, they hauled themselves from their beds, limbs jerking almost as if they were puppets on invisible strings, shambling forwards towards them.

'What's happening?' Jaffa stammered.

Martha was pushing Marisha towards the door. 'Nothing good, now stop dithering and get out.'

Marisha slipped an arm around Ku'ra's waist and half-dragged him out of the ward. Jaffa was surrounded by his former patients now, vainly trying to push them back.

'Come on!' screamed Martha. 'Get out of there! Quickly!'

With shocking suddenness, the young woman who had attacked Marisha lunged forward, her hands grasping Jaffa on each side of his head, tearing away his sterilisation mask. She leant forward and, for one extraordinary moment, Martha thought that she was going to kiss him. Instead the woman gave a rasping cough and exhaled a thin cloud of grey dust that enveloped the unfortunate doctor. He dropped like a stone, face frozen in surprise.

Martha could hear Marisha screaming at her to get out. She turned and hurled herself through the door, landing heavily on the office floor. The glass door slammed shut behind her, Marisha swiping her card frantically through the locking controls. Bolts clunked into place, locking the door solid. The patients started to bang their palms on the door, pressing themselves against the glass, faces contorted in rage, desperate to get out.

ELEVEN

Curtis Rabley zipped the holdall shut and glanced at himself in the mirror, adjusting his dark glasses and wiping the beads of sweat from his brow. Satisfied that no one would give him a second glance amongst the hordes of tourists, he opened the door to his room, checked that the coast was clear and slipped out into the corridor.

Reprogramming the safe timer had taken longer than he had expected, and the longer he stayed in the room the more chance there was of someone finding him.

At one point, the phone next to O'Keefe's bed had rung, and Rabley had practically jumped out of his skin. That was when he'd realised that he was running out of time. If someone was trying to get in touch with O'Keefe, that probably meant that the car had been found. He needed to get out of the dome, and quickly.

The lift arrived, and Rabley hurried inside. As it descended towards the lobby, he forced himself to relax. A lazy smile twitched the corners of his mouth. Despite himself, he was actually starting to enjoy this. Theft had always been like a game to him. A complex game of chess, positioning pieces so that, when the time came, everything was in place for a swift and decisive conclusion.

This game was going his way. All his pieces were in place. All he had to do was make his way to the airport, board a plane and he was away scot-free.

He was looking forward to spending O'Keefe's money. He was fed up with being baking hot on some manicured beach or freezing to death in some crowded ski resort. He'd get himself a nice little place on the west coast of Ireland. A nice pub within walking distance, a nice view of the sea and a nice Irish girl.

His smile broadened. Even if that fool Bunta did suspect that he might have tried something like this, the man certainly didn't have the imagination to look for him somewhere as low-key as Ireland. No, even if they suspected him, Bunta would assume that he'd fled to Cuba, or Vegas or the Bahamas.

When the lift doors opened, Rabley stepped into the foyer with a spring in his step. After a lifetime of people putting him down, Curtis Rabley was finally going to come out on top.

The Doctor slowly made his way along the deserted corridors of SnowGlobe 7, the light from his torch sending shadows dancing across the dusty floor. Behind him, Twelve's methodical footfalls echoed alarmingly, and the Doctor began to wonder about the wisdom of trying to explore stealthily with a two-metre service robot in tow.

He continued to mull over the dozens of possibilities that could account for the presence of the creatures in the ice. He was certain in his own mind that they weren't indigenous. That meant that they came from space. So far they had shown no sign of intelligence beyond an instinct for survival, which meant that they had either been brought to Earth by some other species or had arrived here by accident. On top of that, the ice that they were found in meant that they were old. Very old.

The Doctor sighed. If Stone Age man armed with rocks and clubs had managed to defeat the creatures, then he should have no problem at all. In theory. Perhaps it really was just a matter of intelligence. He was hoping to avoid confrontation and violence. Primitive man would have had no such qualms. A simple case of kill or be killed.

The Doctor knew that scenario only too well. To know that the only way to win was to destroy everything. To be the last of his kind.

He stopped and took a deep breath, clearing the flames of his past from his mind. It did him no good to dwell on things long dead. He needed to focus. The creatures had the ability to operate on some telepathic frequencies. That gave him a way in, he was certain of it.

He had studied the little pad that Roberts has given him, scanning through the schematics of the SnowGlobe. There were two sub-levels. The upper one housed offices and laboratories; the lower one had been given over to storage, server rooms and mechanical workshops. The tunnel where the creatures had first been found was a service corridor on the lowest level, housing shared utilities for the two domes – electrics, water and mile upon mile of fibre-optic connections. They had been running a spur off that tunnel, burrowing up into the ice and bedrock of the preserved Arctic itself when the accident had happened. The Doctor was convinced that returning to the scene of that accident was the key to understanding these creatures.

His torch beam played across a doorway with a sign that read 'Emergency Stairs'. He pushed it open and peered down into the gloom.

'Why is it that I always end up in dark underground passages, eh?'

The robot behind him whirred.

'+UNABLE TO PROVIDE SATISFACTORY ANSWER TO THAT QUESTION.+'

'No, I know the feeling. I've never been able to provide a satisfactory answer myself.'

Torch held out in front of him, the Doctor made his way carefully down the darkened stairwell.

Cowley had watched from the morgue as the patients had risen from their beds hissing and shrieking their fury. Her face had wrinkled in distaste. Those imperfect creatures had no part in the future that she would create, they were resources, fodder, nothing more.

They had, however, given her the distraction that she needed. Harrison was on his feet staring in disbelief at the chaos, barely aware of her as she lifted the heavy metal case containing the eggs into her arms and hurried over to the main doors, swiping her identity card across the reader.

As the doors hissed open, Harrison turned towards her, panicked and flustered.

'Director. What's happening?'

His eyes flicked down to the case in her arms. Confusion flashed across his face, then horror, as he recognised what the case contained.

'What… What are you…?'

Aware that she had lost her element of surprise, Cowley lunged for the door. With surprising speed, Harrison caught her sleeve.

'No! You can't!'

Cowley lashed out, swinging the case with all her might and catching him across the temple. He hit the floor without a sound.

Glancing back at the ward to ensure she hadn't been seen, Cowley slipped out through the doors, locking them behind her, and hurried off along the corridor.

Martha lay breathless and panting on the floor. Marisha was backing away from the door, her hands clasped to her face. 'Dr Jaffa…' whispered the nurse.

Martha scrambled to her feet, catching Marisha by her shoulders. 'He's gone Marisha. He didn't stand a chance.'

Tears ran down the young nurse's face. She couldn't take her eyes off the angry faces on the other side of the glass.

'Will that hold them?' Martha shook her. 'Marisha! Will that door hold them?'

Marisha's gaze snapped back to Martha's face. She wiped the tears from her face, shaking her head. 'It might hold them for a while, but it's designed to stop micro-organisms getting out, not a mob.'

'And it's only a matter of time before one of them decides to chuck a chair through the glass.'

Martha looked at the terrified faces in the medical centre, surprising herself by how calm she felt. Behind her, the glass shuddered under impact after impact. The glass could give way any second.

'All right, everybody out, now!' she ordered. 'We've got to seal this entire section off.'

'Seal it off? Marisha looked shocked. 'You mean just leave them?'

'They're infected,' Martha told her. 'Whatever those things are in the dome, they have infected those people, something in that dust, and if we're not careful they are going to infect everyone in this dome. We've got to set up barriers, quarantine them.'

She pulled off the sterilisation device from behind her ear. 'How many more of these have we got?'

'I'm not sure.' Marisha looked over at a glass-fronted cupboard mounted on the wall. 'Fifteen, maybe twenty. Probably more down in the stores.'

'All right then, get them, make sure everyone here has got one. Mr Harrison...?' Martha looked round for him.

Harrison was face down by the main doors, an ugly gash across his forehead.

'Mr Harrison!' Martha hurried over to him.

Ku'ra helped her lift him back onto the bench. The Welshman groaned weakly.

Marisha tilted Harrison's head back to examine the

wound, all panic banished now that she was faced with a patient. 'We'll need to get that cleaned.'

'What happened?' asked Martha.

Harrison winced as Marisha applied a sterilised pad to his head. 'It was the Director.'

'Cowley?'

'She hit me.' Harrison's eyes widened. 'She had the case. The eggs!'

'What?' Martha stared at him in disbelief.

Ku'ra tried the doors. 'She's locked us in!'

Martha cursed under her breath. She had known that something was wrong with Cowley, so had the Doctor. They should have done something about her earlier. She was unstable and dangerous and, if the Doctor was right, the Director now had the means to infect every animal on the planet.

Martha joined Ku'ra at the door, poking uselessly at the locked door control.

'We've got to stop her. We've got to get those eggs back.'

A splintering crash from the ward made them turn. One of the patients was swinging a chair again and again at the window. A spider's web of cracks was spreading across the toughened glass.

Ku'ra shook his head. 'We need to worry about ourselves first.'

'We've got the sterilisation masks.'

'You think that's going to help us? You saw what they did to Jaffa. If they get anywhere near us, we'll be contaminated.'

Martha stared helplessly around. There was no way out. The only doors led to Jaffa's office or the morgue.

She gripped Ku'ra's arm. 'The morgue.'

'What?'

'It's solid. They'll never get through that door.'

'We'll be trapped, Martha!'

With a terrifying crash, the window to the ward gave way and the patients spilled out in a spitting tide of bodies.

'No choice!' Martha dragged Ku'ra with her as the patients surged towards them. Martha kicked out, sending the hospital gurney sailing across the room. It cannoned into the patients, sending them toppling like skittles. The thing that had once been Dr Al-Bakri scrabbled forward, grasping Marisha by the hair. Harrison batted uselessly at him. With a bellow, Martha threw herself forward, catching him in the solar plexus with her elbow and sending him crashing to the ground.

She hauled Marisha to her feet. 'Come on! Ku'ra, you get Harrison.'

Kicking out at the grasping hands, the four of them dived through the open door of the morgue, Ku'ra pulling it shut with a deafening clang. They could hear fingers scratching on the metal.

'Lock it, lock it!' screamed Marisha.

Ku'ra punched at the keypad, and there was a reassuring clunk. Martha dropped onto her haunches, breathing heavily. Ku'ra shot her a nervous grin.

'Well, Dr Jones. We're safe for the moment. Now what do we do?'

Martha shook her head in frustration. 'Hope that it takes them longer to get out through the main doors than it did for them to get out of the ward! Doesn't anyone believe in solid doors in this place?'

'I don't suppose anyone expected them to be keeping a bunch of homicidal patients from getting out,' said Ku'ra.

Martha looked at him thoughtfully. 'Quite desperate to get out in fact.' She looked back at the sea of people scrabbling at the ward door. 'Where do you suppose they're trying to get to?'

Ku'ra shrugged. 'Dunno. Just out.'

Martha shook her head. 'No, there's more to it than that. This all started right after you felt something in your head. Something telepathic, right?'

'A signal?'

'Exactly! A mental signal of some kind.'

'Do you mean that that creature is talking to them in some way, controlling them by some kind of mental remote control?' Harrison was looking at her with a new respect.

Ku'ra frowned. 'You're kidding, right?'

'Why not! We know the creature is telepathic in some way. We know that it has infected these people with the dust from its eggs.'

'But that would mean that all those people are probably trying to get to…' Marisha tailed off.

'The other dome.' Martha felt sick. 'The creature doesn't come out and hunt its food, it makes sure that its food comes to it.'

'There are nearly eight hundred people in this dome.'

Ku'ra's face was a very pale shade of blue. 'If they get out, or if Cowley opens that case…'

Martha's face was grim. Somewhere out there, Director Cowley was loose with a biological time bomb, and they were trapped here with the infected.

The Doctor emerged from the stairwell into a long, low corridor that curved, like all the others in the building, in a gentle arc. Unlike the public areas, everything here was dull, grey concrete, the ceilings festooned with pipes and wiring. Gingerly, he felt for a light switch. Flickering and buzzing strip lights juddered into life, throwing harsh shadows across the walls.

He peered at a cluster of signs that hung untidily from a metal beam in the ceiling. An arrow indicated that the entrance to the maintenance tunnel was about a hundred metres along the corridor to his left.

He started towards it, then stopped, aware that he was suddenly on his own. Twelve was motionless at the base the stairwell. The Doctor could hear a frantic whirr as hard drives spun into life.

'What is it, Twelve?' he hissed.

'+THIS PLACE IS… FAMILIAR.+'

The Doctor hurried back to it. 'Yes, that's right.'

'+THERE IS DANGER. YOU SHOULD NOT BE HERE.+'

'We've no choice, Twelve.'

'+THERE IS DANGER.+'

'I know!' The Doctor tried to hush the agitated robot.

'+I DO NOT WISH TO BE RESPONSIBLE FOR THE

DEATHS OF ANY MORE HUMANS,+' it told him. '+I AM PROGRAMMED TO PROTECT. YOU SHOULD NOT BE HERE.+'

'Yes, but..'

'+I AM… FRIGHTENED.+'

The Doctor looked up in surprise. 'Twelve, listen to me. I'm frightened too, but people are depending on us. Lots of people. All of the humans in the other dome, all of the humans outside. You know where the accident took place. I need you to show me. Do you understand?'

The robot nodded slowly. '+I UNDERSTAND.+'

It straightened, its head turning smoothly in a complete circle, lights blinking on the panel on its chest.

'+I AM DETECTING A CONCENTRATION OF LIFE FORMS 227 YARDS TO MY LEFT.+'

The Doctor nodded grimly. 'That's what we've come to find.'

'+ONE OF THE LIFE SIGNS IS HUMAN.+'

TWELVE

As Rabley approached the main airlock doors of SnowGlobe 6, he could see that a crowd had formed; quite a large crowd at that. He frowned. Instead of the usual background babble of excited holidaymakers, he could hear raised, angry voices.

He stopped. There was no way he could get to the exit, there must have been forty or fifty people clustered around the airlock doors. More worrying, the doors themselves were shut, a tourist coach stuck on the exit ramp, the driver shrugging and gesturing at the closed doors as a dozen or so tourists chattered animatedly at him.

Rabley skirted around the back of the crowd, not wanting to draw attention to himself but desperate to find out what was going on. He couldn't believe he had got this close. Only the doors stood between him and freedom.

A long balcony area surrounded the coach park inside the doors, a meeting point where people waited to greet new arrivals or see off departures. Rabley scampered up the short stairs, pushing through the half a dozen people gathered there, ignoring their grunts of indignation as he forced his way to the railing. Immediately, he had to fight down the urge to turn and run. Standing in front of the main doors of the SnowGlobe were half a dozen armed security personnel led by a tall bearded man – Hassan, was it? Rabley seemed to remember him from when he and O'Keefe had arrived. There were at least a dozen more guards scattered along the rim of the dome. Rabley had been around in enough similar situations to see that the guards were jittery, fingers hovering over triggers. The crowd seemed oblivious to that fact.

Rabley tried to slow his breathing, aware that he was starting to sweat. This couldn't possibly be about him. They couldn't possibly have had time to work out that he had survived the attack in the SnowGlobe.

He strained to hear what was being said. The tourist who seemed to be the self-appointed leader of the growing mob was German, or at least spoke with a heavy Germanic accent. He was purple with rage, demanding to know why he was being barred from leaving the dome.

The security leader regarded him with barely disguised contempt, waiting until the man had finished his diatribe before calmly raising his microphone.

'If I might have your attention once again.' Captain Hassan's voice boomed from speakers set over the door. 'As I have explained to you, a situation has arisen that has made it necessary to seal the dome for a short period. The matter is one of security, and I am not at liberty to divulge its nature at the present time. For your own safety, I must ask you to return to your hotel rooms or chalets. Facilities inside the dome will continue as normal, but for the time being I must ask that you assist the security services and do not attempt to leave the dome. Now I must please ask you to disperse quietly and in an orderly manner.'

An angry tide of voices rose from the crowd once more, cut dead as the security captain pointedly raised his rifle. 'Please have no illusions about the seriousness with which I make this request. Anyone attempting to force their way out, or impeding my men in any way will be arrested.'

There was a moment of shocked silence. The German couldn't have looked more angry if he had tried, and for a moment Rabley honestly thought that the man was going to try and tackle the security captain with his bare hands. Fortunately, his ample wife hauling on his arm brought him to his senses, her eyes never leaving the captain's rifle, and the man reluctantly allowed himself to be led away.

Rabley leant on the railing, his mind racing. He was certain now that this wasn't about him – it was probably a security exercise of some kind – but that didn't help matters. Every minute he remained in the dome was a minute where he might be recognised, and if that happened then his entire plan came crashing down around his ears.

As he turned, intending to tuck himself into a corner of one of the quieter bars until this security alert was over, a figure stepped in front of him. Rabley glanced up and froze.

Director Cowley was standing on the balcony less than a metre from him, staring down into the grumbling crowd, a large metal case in her arms.

Rabley started to back away, praying that she wouldn't see him. Even with his 'disguise', he had spent too long around the woman for the last few days for her not to recognise him. His heart was pounding. If he could just get down the stairs and into the surge of milling tourists…

Cowley turned and looked him full in the face.

Rabley stopped, like a rabbit caught in headlights, his dreams of living out a quiet, idyllic existence dispersing like the crowd. For what seemed like an eternity she stared at him, then, miraculously, she turned and walked away.

Rabley watched her go, unable to believe that she hadn't realised who he was. But there had been no recognition on her face. Truth be told, there had been nothing in her face, no expression whatsoever. It was almost as if she was stunned, or drugged.

Puzzled, Rabley watched as the Director weaved her way through the rapidly thinning crowd. Surely, if there was a security alert, she should be involved in some way. Yet she had been staring at the closed gates as if she was as bemused as the tourists around her. As she hurried away, she kept checking over her shoulder, almost as if she was anxious that the security teams didn't see her. She clutched the metal case hard to her chest as if her life depended on it. His curiosity getting the better of him, Rabley followed her, keeping a discreet distance.

Cowley turned off from the main path, ducking under a sign that said 'Authorised Personnel Only' and busying herself at a security pad set into the dome wall next to a heavy steel door. She vanished inside, and Rabley hurried over, catching the door before it swung closed.

Cautiously, he peered inside. Metal steps led down to a long service corridor. He could smell fuel oil and musty warm air. Cowley was out of sight, but Rabley could hear the click of her heels echoing down the corridor.

Rabley rubbed his chin. He didn't like changing his plans on the hoof, but he certainly wasn't going to get out through the main doors carrying a bag with nearly a million dollars whilst there were armed security guards stomping about. Besides, there was a faint chance that this might lead him to an alternative way out...

Mind made up, he quickly checked to make sure that no one had seen him, then slipped through the door after Cowley.

The Doctor picked his way carefully through the wreckage that littered the tunnel floor. The service corridor was a mess of broken equipment and jagged chunks of ice and rock. He was nearing the site of the accident.

The tunnel ahead of him was dark, the few lights that were still functioning strewn across the frozen ground, casting long shadows up the walls. The tunnel itself was a mess and huge sections of the ceiling had given way, revealing long, dark chasms stretching deep overhead, the rock frosted and glittering with ice. Here and there were the broken twisted limbs of service robots, their metal bodies still buried under tons of rubble.

The Doctor had left Service Robot Twelve back along the corridor for the time being. Hassan had been right, the robot's positronic mind was in a very fragile state and, desperate as he was for information, the Doctor didn't want to run the risk of causing a complete breakdown. He had no idea if the robot would react as a human might when confronted with half a dozen corpses. It was difficult to tell. Artificial intelligence was a very complicated science, even for him.

He stopped to examine one of the fallen robots. The salvage team had obviously made a start at trying to recover as much equipment as they could, they couldn't have had more than a couple of minutes before they succumbed to the dust given off from the eggs.

He shone the light from his torch over the shattered walls, muttering to himself. 'If this is where the accident happened then somewhere around here should be… Ah-ha!'

Light glanced off a jagged fissure in the ice, a great tear that went from floor to ceiling. The floor was treacherously slippery, glassy and smooth like an ice rink where the ice had melted and then refrozen. Cautiously the Doctor edged forward. He peered into the crack in the ice. The fissure was narrow, but seemed to open up further along. He squeezed himself into the narrow gap, gasping as the cold leeched through his clothes. There was just enough room for him to ease himself forward.

As he edged his way deeper and deeper into the passageway, he became aware of shapes behind the frozen surface, rocks embedded deep in the ice, their surfaces alive with ancient pictures. The Doctor squinted, trying to make out the details, but the thick ice distorted everything.

Abruptly, the passageway opened out. The Doctor stopped, staring in wonder at the images in the rock that arced overhead, images that had remained hidden for centuries, that might never have been found if human beings hadn't been desperate to preserve the wilderness of their world.

He craned his neck back, trying to get a better look at the paintings. Like all prehistoric art, there was ritual as well as storytelling involved. There might be something in the pictures that could help him.

A harsh clicking made him freeze. Ahead of him, he could see a dark shadow moving stealthily along the fissure, long spider-like legs scraping on the ice.

The Doctor pressed himself hard against the wall as one of the creatures emerged into the opening, clinging tight to the ceiling, head moving to and fro. It stopped, hanging there like some huge spider on the ceiling, ice splintering noisily where its claws dug in.

The Doctor was torn between his instinct to run and finally having the ability to study one of the creatures up close. It really did seem to comprise of all the parts of a creature from nightmare. The heavy, swollen body quivered under pockmarked skin that was swathed in thick wiry fur. The fleshy, bat-like nose was wrinkled and wet, thick trails of mucus stringing off it. Each of the eight legs was long and bony, stiff bristles squeaking shrilly as they brushed against each other. The front two legs ended in two long, sinuous, strangely elegant fingers, constantly touching and feeling their surroundings.

The creature seemed jittery and nervous, its movements clumsy and unsure. With a sudden shock, the Doctor realised that it was a newborn, a recent addition to what must have been an ever-growing number of these creatures.

The grasping hands reached out, and the Doctor had to duck as long, bristle-covered fingers poked and prodded at the rock behind him. He held his breath as the creature's digits picked and pawed at the frozen surface, pushing into crevices and cracks. Finding no food, it let out an angry hiss and, in a shower of splintering ice, scuttled past him out into the service corridor. The Doctor let out his breath in a rush. He could hear the rattle of the creature's echo-location and the squeal of a rat as it finally located some prey.

He started gently edging his way down the passageway from which the creature had come. Ahead of him, a low, insistent noise started to build, a constant staccato chattering, like a field full of crickets on a summer's day. Behind the noise, right on the very edge of his perception, the Doctor was aware of another sound, something that he could hear with his mind rather than his ears. It wasn't a nice sensation.

Gritting his teeth, the Doctor pushed forward. The passageway had narrowed again, but he was certain he could see where it ended. A dull, bluish light was spilling back along the fissure.

He crept to the mouth of the passageway and peered out. Before him was a vast cavern, a cathedral of huge frozen shapes carved in the ice. Light filtered down through narrow tears in the roof, throwing long shafts of brightness across the icy floor.

In the centre of the cavern, picked out in the slashes of

light, a huge creature sat like some vast, bloated Buddha. Each of its eight arms was wrapped around its huge black body, long fingers flexing and kneading at the thick, blubbery flesh. It swayed slowly, moving back and forth in time with its stentorian breathing, wet nose flickering and pulsing. Half a dozen of its young scampered around it, clicking and mewing, batting at each other viciously if they came within touching distance, occasionally darting away, but always returning to lurk in the shadow of the huge, quivering bulk.

The Doctor felt his hearts sink. Six young. If three of those were the ones that had hatched from the eggs they already knew about then the others had to have hatched from either Brian Williams, the security team or Maxwell O'Keefe and his assistant. That there weren't more than six of the creatures meant that either the security team had managed to destroy some of them, or that not everyone had been used as a host. The Doctor gritted his teeth. The creatures were carnivorous, he just hoped that they occasionally took their food back to keep in the larder.

He winced as another wave of mental energy wafted across him. The creature's mind was getting stronger and stronger, and he was beginning to understand the relationship between the creature and the comatose patients back in the sick bay. He had to find a weakness in these things, and quickly.

Concentrating, he started to focus his mind, intending to relax his telepathic barriers for a fraction of a second, letting the creature's consciousness touch his, trying to see if there was anything in its design that he could reach.

The mental surge caught him totally unprepared. Suddenly his mind was full of rage and pain and hunger and an overwhelming desire to give himself up to the things in the cavern below.

Reeling, the Doctor staggered back, desperately trying to hang on to consciousness as his mind closed down, defence systems shutting out the mental hold of the creature. His vision blurred and he lost his footing on the icy rock. Limbs like lead, the Doctor felt himself pitch forward, falling headlong, then he knew nothing.

THIRTEEN

Martha sat on the floor, her back against the cold metal wall of the morgue, listening to the sounds of destruction that raged outside the door. She couldn't recall ever feeling so helpless. The patients had failed to break their way out of the medical bay, that much was clear. But she and the others were effectively prisoners for as long as the patients were out there, and she knew that Cowley was getting further and further away with every minute that passed. Ku'ra was pacing the room, angry at finding himself trapped. Harrison just stood there wringing his hands with worry, jumping at every unfamiliar noise from outside the doors.

Martha jumped herself as a particularly loud thump made the door shudder.

'What if they get in?' said Harrison nervously.

Marisha shook her head. 'They won't.'

'They got out of the ward.'

'That was a glass door. This is different.'

The door shook again from a series of heavy blows. Harrison shuffled backwards towards the corner of the room. 'I hope you're right.'

Marisha slid down the wall to sit next to Martha. 'He's right you know,' she whispered conspiratorially. 'This door wasn't designed to be sealed from the inside. If Jaffa remembers the right sequence on the door release…'

Martha shook her head. 'They didn't look as though they were acting rationally to me. I don't think they're still thinking like normal people. If Ku'ra is right then they're operating on the most basic of levels, just one thought in their frenzied little heads. Get to the other dome and hand yourself over to be eaten.'

'Infecting everyone they pass on the way.'

Martha grimaced, remembering the cloud of choking dust that had spewed from the mouths of the infected patients, and how fast Jaffa had succumbed. What was it the Doctor had said? A pandemic that could infect the entire planet. She had let Cowley escape. She had let the Doctor down. She had let everyone down.

There was a thump from the far side of the room and a muffled curse came from Ku'ra. Martha looked up. 'What's up?'

Ku'ra kicked at a bundle on the floor. 'Tripped over this blasted bio-suit.'

Marisha stared at him. 'What did you say?'

'I said that people should put stuff away and not leave it on the floor for people to trip over. Aren't these things meant to be put in a sterilised locker or something?'

Marisha scrambled to her feet and hurried over to where

Ku'ra was rubbing his shin. On the floor in an untidy pile was the biohazard suit. She snatched it up.

'It's Jaffa's. He was wearing it when he and the Doctor were examining the eggs,' said Marisha. 'I told him that they weren't meant to be worn outside the lab, but he was struggling with the case and I wasn't in the mood to argue with him.'

'OK, sure, but what use is that to us?' asked Martha.

Marisha pointed at a small tag sewn into the sleeve. 'It's an emergency override for the doors. We can get out.'

Martha grinned at her.

Ku'ra shook his head. 'Now hang on a minute. There's only one suit.'

'Only one of us has to go after Cowley.' Martha's face was grave.

'Forget it, Martha. Open that door, they'll be all over you.'

Martha plucked the little sterilisation headset from behind her ear. 'Look, these have been the only protection that we've had, right? And they're no use against those people out there 'cos they can just tear them off, but this...' She held up the bio-suit with its bulky helmet. 'They'll never get through this. Not without a lot of effort. I have to go after her. I have to stop her.'

'You're not suggesting that we let those things in here, just so that you can escape?' Harrison's voice was shrill and trembling.

'You heard what the Doctor said. If she opens that case then *everyone* is infected.'

There was silence in the morgue for a long while, then

Ku'ra gave a grim smile. 'Sounds like we've got a plan. Let's do it.'

Ignoring the protests of Mr Harrison, Martha started to struggle into the bulky bio-suit.

Rabley hurried along the long corridor, hugging the shadows against the wall, keeping Cowley in sight without risking being seen himself. Rabley hadn't realised that the sub-levels were so extensive. If he lost her down here, he'd have a devil of a job finding her again, or finding his way back out.

Cowley had a specific destination in mind, of that Rabley had no doubt. Her movements were too precise, too deliberate for this to be some random journey into the bowels of the facility. She moved at a brisk pace, and more than once Rabley had had to proceed faster than he would have liked in order to keep up with her.

He stepped through a doorway into a corridor that was wide and straight, seemingly stretching on indefinitely. Cowley's slim form wandered in and out of the pools of flickering, intermittent light from the fluorescent tubes that hung from the low ceiling.

Rabley looked around, his brow furrowing. Mr O'Keefe had mentioned an accident that had occurred in some tunnels underneath the SnowGlobe. But if that was where they were, then…

Rabley's heart started pounding as he realised that Cowley had led him down to the service corridor that connected the two SnowGlobes. If he followed Cowley down this corridor then he was going to end up right back where he started. In SnowGlobe 7 with those... monsters.

Rabley stopped, gripped by a sudden urge to turn and run, to put the money back in the safe and forget about his bold plan altogether. Cowley couldn't possibly know what she was walking into.

He felt a sudden pang of guilt. Could he really just leave and let the woman walk into the arms of those things? Rabley punched the wall angrily. He had been so close...

He focused on the multitude of warning signs and health and safety instructions that decorated the wall, trying to calm himself down. One particular sign made him stop and stare, and a broad smile started spreading slowly across his face.

'In Event of Emergency Use Ventilator Shaft as Exit.' He read the words out loud, unable to believe his luck.

Cowley wasn't heading for the other dome at all. She was heading for the ventilator shaft. Hefting the bag of money up onto his shoulder, Rabley hurried to catch up with her.

The first thing the Doctor was aware of was the smell – a ripe, all-pervading smell of rotting meat. Groggily, he forced his eyes open, his nose wrinkling in distaste. He was flat on his back, staring at the icy ceiling, snowflakes drifting through the cracks in the roof and landing wetly on his cheeks.

He struggled to raise his head, and wondered how he'd managed to survive the fall without breaking his neck. The entrance to the fissure he had fallen from was about four metres above him. As his elbows sank into something bristly and soft, the Doctor realised that his fall had been broken by the dead and bloated body of one of the creatures.

With a cry of disgust, he rolled himself off the spongy corpse, staggering unsteadily to his feet. His head was still pounding, and he weaved unsteadily for a moment as he struggled to regain his balance. He'd been totally unprepared for the raw, primal force of the creature's thoughts. 'Stupid, Doctor. Really, really stupid,' he muttered to himself.

Shaking his head to try and clear the lingering fuzziness he felt, the Doctor looked around at his surroundings. He was in a pit gouged in the ice, the walls stained with red. In the gloom, he could make out bodies: one was the creature he had fallen onto; the others were a more familiar shape, their outlines softened by the gently falling snow.

Grimacing at the unpleasantness of his task, the Doctor made a swift examination of the corpses in the pit. The body of the creature was nearly half-eaten, but the cause of death had clearly been an automatic weapon of some kind. Ragged holes were torn in the thick fur, the edges caked with dried blood. Clearly, the things had no problem with cannibalising their own kind.

What was left of the other bodies showed no sign of gunshot wounds, just ragged tears that could only have been caused by the frenzied attack of a predator. In all four cases, the bodies were only partial. The Doctor's face was grim, knowing full well what had become of the missing parts. The four victims had been used both as food and as hosts.

The Doctor straightened. He was too late to do anything for these people, but Twelve had detected a human life sign and, unless any other unfortunates had stumbled into the claws of the creatures, that could only be Maxwell O'Keefe or his assistant.

The Doctor peered around the gloomy pit, aware of the scuffling and clicking from the cave, and of how dangerous his position had become. To one side of the pit the drifting snow had formed a large mound. There was a leg sticking out from underneath it. Tentatively, the Doctor started to dig at the mound of snow. His fingers brushed against something clammy and wet. Crouching down on his haunches, he raised his torch. There was a face in the soft snow, the features made nightmarish and grotesque by the harsh white light.

'Maxwell O'Keefe, I presume.'

The Doctor reached down, feeling for a pulse in the man's neck. As his fingers touched O'Keefe's skin, the man practically exploded from the snow, eyes bulging and wide.

The Doctor tumbled backwards, caught completely off-guard.

O'Keefe clawed at him, like a man possessed. The Doctor desperately tried to calm him, but the big man was strong and panic-stricken. A flailing hand caught in the strap hanging from the Doctor's neck, snapping it and sending the sonic screwdriver tumbling to the floor.

The Doctor watched in horror as the slim tube hit the ice with a hard clunk.

And shut off.

From above them there was a sudden violent barrage of clicks and whistles and the sound of dozens of spidery limbs clattering across the ice.

Snow and splintered ice showered down around the Doctor's head. He looked up to see the creatures looming over the rim of the pit, bat-like noses wrinkling and twitching, thick drool splattering on the floor.

In unison, all six creatures bared their razor sharp teeth and shrieked in fury.

Martha stood in front of the morgue door, trying to calm her breathing, which was starting to mist up the faceplate of the clumsy bio-suit. The air in the suit was stale and musty; there had been no way of recharging the oxygen bottles strung across her back. Marisha had estimated that she had ten minutes of air at most. That didn't worry Martha too much: if she didn't manage to get out of the medical bay in ten minutes, the chances were that she'd be better off suffocating.

'You OK in there?' Ku'ra's voice was muffled and muted through the helmet.

Martha gave him a thumbs-up. The young Flisk looked as nervous as she felt. She couldn't blame him. As soon as they opened the doors, he'd be fighting for his life.

On the far side of the room, Marisha was trying to keep Harrison under control. The Welshman was terrified. Martha had a horrible feeling that of all the things that could go wrong, Harrison might turn out to be the most unpredictable element of all.

Marisha gave Ku'ra a subtle nod. Harrison had finally

calmed down. If they were going to do it, then now was the time.

Ku'ra squeezed Martha's arm. 'You be careful out there.'

Martha braced herself. Once the door was open, she was simply intending to run headlong until she reached the main exit. Then she just hoped that she could fight the patients off long enough for the chip in the suit to get the door unlocked. She hefted the aluminium chair leg that she held, uncomfortable with the weapon. Ku'ra had insisted that she took it. The patients showed no remorse at the damage they inflicted in their need to escape, so she had to be equally single-minded.

Ku'ra had his ear pressed to the door, listening to the sounds from outside, trying to time the moment for maximum advantage. Abruptly, he straightened and gripped the door handle.

'This is it, here we go!'

As Ku'ra deactivated the lock and hauled open the heavy door, Martha launched herself forward, head down, arms tucked in against her sides. At the very same moment, Harrison pulled himself loose from Marisha and threw himself at the opening door, screaming hysterically.

Taken completely by surprise, Ku'ra gave a grunt of pain as the little man barrelled into him. He lost his footing on the smooth floor, and the two of them crashed into the door. Their combined weight slammed it into Martha's shoulder. Her arms flailed wildly as she struggled to stay upright, but the cumbersome biohazard suit hadn't been built for athletics.

She crashed to the floor, skidding into the ward. At once, a dozen twisted, angry faces turned in her direction. Winded, Martha tried to catch her breath. She could hear Ku'ra screaming at her to get up. She caught hold of the edge of the reception desk, trying to haul herself upright. With an angry scream, the patients surged forward. Martha lashed out with the chair leg. There was a dull thump as it connected with one of the flailing bodies, and a patient crashed to the floor.

Martha felt hands dragging her to her feet. Through the visor in the helmet she could see nothing but angry screaming faces. A woman loomed close, lips curled back in a savage snarl. A cloud of grey dust billowed from her mouth, obscuring Martha's view. She lashed out blindly, hearing her heavy glove connect with something soft, and the grip of the grasping hands slackened momentarily. She pulled herself free, backing herself up against the wall, swinging the chair leg in a wide arc.

The medical bay was in chaos. Furniture and equipment lay in shattered piles, medical files and printouts strewn everywhere. The ward itself was a jumble of upturned beds and broken glass. Amazingly, the door out to the rest of the building and the window in Jaffa's office were unbroken. Whoever had built this place had done their job properly.

There was a frightened scream from the other side of the ward. Dr Jaffa and three of the other infected people were clustered around the door to the morgue. Martha could see Ku'ra, Harrison and Marisha struggling to pull it shut. Two of the patients had managed get a grip on

Harrison's jacket and were hauling him through the gap. His face was a mask of terror as he desperately tried to hang on to Marisha's arm. There was a cloud of black dust, and Harrison vanished into the throng with a strangled cry. Snarling, Jaffa gripped the lip of the door. Inch by inch, he hauled it open. They would be in the morgue in moments.

Martha tried to focus on the exit. Her vision blurred. It was getting harder to breathe. Her exertions were using up the oxygen faster than she had expected. The chair leg was starting to feel heavy.

She swung it again at the patients encircling her and felt it slip from her grasp. Shouting with frustration, she tried to force her way through the angry crowd, but the weight of numbers dragged her to the floor.

Choking, Martha could feel hands on her chest, around her neck. She tried to draw in breath but nothing came.

Harrison had been right, they didn't stand a chance.

She had failed.

FOURTEEN

The Doctor snatched up the sonic screwdriver and
climbed slowly to his feet, backing away from the
creatures. One of them hissed angrily, clambering down
the side of the pit like a vast spider. The Doctor fumbled
with the screwdriver's controls, knowing that he had
no chance of resetting his sonic camouflage before the
creatures had a hold of him. Long fingers were already
stretching out for him.

He closed his eyes as fingertips brushed across his face.
A low rumble started to reverberate through the cavern.
Abruptly, the probing fingers withdrew. The Doctor opened
one eye. Snow and shards of ice were being shaken from
the pit wall. The creatures were backing away, nervous and
agitated. The rumbling got louder and louder then, with
an explosion of ice and rock, something huge and metallic
burst through the ice wall and into the cavern.

The creatures scattered as rock and ice tumbled to
the floor. The Doctor grabbed O'Keefe by the collar and,

with superhuman effort, hauled the big man to one side as Service Robot Twelve landed with a deafening crash in the centre of the pit. At once, the creatures launched themselves forward, spitting their fury at the intruder that was keeping them from their prey. Twelve batted at them with huge metallic arms, pistons hissing. The creatures tumbled like skittles, skidding across the ice, mewling and chittering.

The robot hauled itself out of the pit, ice splintering under its feet. The creatures circled it warily, snarling and spitting, the clicks and pops from their echo-location reverberating around the cavern. One of them leapt onto Twelve's back, claws scrabbling on the smooth metal. The robot twisted, catching hold of one of the creature's spindly legs and swinging it high into the air.

The creature bellowed its anger as the robot twirled it like some bizarre bolas. The cries were cut short with a horrible wet popping noise as Twelve smashed it onto the hard ice.

The cavern was immediately filled with a cacophony of screeching and snarling. Above the noise, the Doctor could hear something deeper, more malevolent. Roused from its telepathic trance by the death cries of its young, the parent creature unfolded itself slowly, long powerful legs lifting its bristle-covered bulk from the ice.

Towering over Twelve, it let out a deafening roar and swiped out with razor-sharp claws.

In the medical bay, it was if someone had flicked off a switch.

There was a moment of sudden shocking silence, and Martha felt the hands that had threatened to choke the life out of her go limp. All around her, the patients simply dropped to the floor like rag dolls.

She struggled to her feet, gloved hands struggling with the clasp at her throat. The helmet came free with a pop. Martha checked that her sterilisation earpiece was still in place and drew in great lungfuls of air. Marisha and Ku'ra peered out in astonishment from the morgue. Jaffa and the others had fallen in an untidy heap at the base of the door, and it took the two of them to force it open far enough to step out.

Outside in the corridor, two security guards suddenly stepped from the lift. They stopped, staring in shock at the scene in front of them, then hurried forward banging on the glass of the door. Martha waved at them angrily. 'All right, all right. Wait a minute can't you? Talk about turning up just *after* the nick of time.'

'What happened?' Marisha was scurrying from patient to patient turning those that had fallen face down, attending to those that had injured themselves as they fell. She looked sadly down at Mr Harrison, his face still frozen in an expression of surprise and fear.

Martha shook her head, 'I don't know. One minute they were all over me, the next...' She looked around at the fallen bodies. 'It's like someone cut the strings.'

'I think that's exactly what happened.' Ku'ra was at her shoulder, rubbing at his temples. 'The telepathic signal, it's back to what it was before. That urge to get to the other dome? I can't feel that any more.'

Martha frowned. 'But that means that the creature has stopped calling them.'

Ku'ra nodded. 'I think it's been distracted by something.'

'I think you mean distracted by some*one*.' Martha chewed her lip nervously. 'What the hell are you up to, Doctor?'

Rabley stared down the long empty corridor stretching ahead of him and cursed under his breath. He had hurried to catch up with the Director, but hadn't been overly concerned about finding her. After all, they were out of the labyrinth of tunnels and stairwells now. The tunnel ran straight to the other SnowGlobe, there was nowhere else she could go.

Now, with the corridor stretching away in front of him and with no sign of Cowley, no noise of her heels clicking on the concrete, it was becoming obvious that he had missed her somewhere. He cursed himself for his lack of concentration. There had to be a side passageway, something he had missed.

Rabley retraced his steps, eyes darting from side to side, peering at signs and notices, looking for anything that might give him a clue as to where she had gone.

A noise made him stop. A scrape of metal. He edged slowly forward, straining to try and locate the source of the sound. It was close.

Something splashed onto his shoulder. He wiped at it absently with his hand. His fingers came away sticky. Rabley grimaced. It was oil. He looked up. There was a hatch set into the ceiling, practically invisible amongst the pipes and cables. The illuminated signs that were meant to indicate its position were dark and caked with dust. No wonder he had missed it.

A ladder in the wall led to a narrow walkway lodged amongst the tangle of pipes. Rabley hoisted his bag onto his shoulder and scrambled up the ladder peer cautiously into the ventilator shaft. The hatch had been propped open, revealing a long, narrow chute, heading upwards at a forty-five-degree angle. Oil dripped from a badly maintained hydraulic pump set into the wall. Hearing the sound of scraping metal again, Rabley nodded in satisfaction. He had found Cowley again.

He ducked into the shaft, swinging the holdall around onto his back and climbing as quickly as he dared. The surface of the shaft was slick with grease. More than once, Rabley had to stop himself from slipping backwards.

The angle of the shaft abruptly lessened as it opened out into a fan room of some kind. On the other side of the room there was a small, square opening leading on to where the shaft continued upwards. Rabley scrambled into the fan room gratefully, his back cracking and protesting as he straightened.

With shock, he realised that Cowley was standing next to the hatchway.

Panicked, Rabley started to back down the shaft, knowing in his heart that it was probably too late but holding on to the one faint hope that she still might not see him. He was not a violent man, but he knew that if the Director recognised him he would have very few choices open to him if he still intended to escape with O'Keefe's money. He prayed it wouldn't come to that.

Slowly, he edged backwards. The Director was still standing amongst the huge fans, bolt upright, stock still, arms by her side, the heavy metal case at her feet. Her head was cocked on one side and there was a puzzled expression on her face. She gave no indication that she had seen him.

Rabley frowned. Cowley looked for all the world as if she was drugged, or sleepwalking. Her face had a slackness to it, her eyes were unfocused. Abruptly, she turned her head and looked straight at Rabley.

'I can't hear them any more.' The Director's voice was faint and childlike. 'Not properly.' She showed no sign that she recognised him at all. 'At first I thought that they could only talk to me, but now, if I concentrate really hard…' She screwed up her eyes. 'I can talk to them…'

A broad smile spread across her face. 'Soon… It will all be over soon.'

With that she turned, picked up the case in her arms and ducked through a hatchway on the far side of the fan room.

Rabley was unable to believe his luck. 'Bonkers. She's completely bonkers.'

He grinned. Even if she *had* recognised him, he doubted that anyone was going to take the Director seriously any more. His grin faded as a thick grille slammed down over the doorway that Cowley had just disappeared through.

'No!'

He hurled himself at the grille, shaking the steel bars uselessly.

On the other side, Cowley was pressing a sequence of buttons on a small control panel, engaging the locks, sealing him in.

'They're coming. Soon you will understand them too.'

Rabley watched helplessly as the Director turned and started to make her way up the shaft towards the surface. He called after her.

'Please, wait. I've got money. We can make a deal.'

The Director didn't turn around. There was a low whine of motors as the fans suddenly started to spin into life. Rabley had to shout to hear himself over the noise, pleading with her to come back, but eventually the sound of the fans drowned him out completely.

He slumped back onto the floor, angry and frustrated. He clamped his hands over his ears, trying to shut out the noise of the fans, forcing himself to think. He couldn't give up now, he couldn't.

Another noise suddenly cut through the low throb of the fans. A harsh insistent clicking that Rabley could feel in his gut. With a chill of horror, he realised that he recognised the sound.

One of the creatures was climbing up the ventilation shaft behind him.

He was trapped.

The parent creature hit Twelve like a steamroller, sending the robot crashing backwards. The Doctor only just managed to haul O'Keefe out of the way as the two giants twisted and thrashed in the bottom of the pit. Ice and snow flew into the air as the creature tore at the steel shell of the robot, but Twelve gripped the creature in huge metal hands, holding it at bay.

The robot staggered slowly to its feet, the thrashing creature gripped tightly in its arms. With a whine of motors, it hurled the creature across the cavern, the huge bulk shattering a vast column of ice and rock that stretched high overhead.

The creature's young scattered as chunks of the ceiling crashed down around them, glittering needles of ice bouncing and spiralling.

Twelve spun round to face the Doctor. '+YOU MUST LEAVE.+'

'No,' snapped the Doctor. 'I'm not leaving, not without you.'

'+YOU MUST.+'

'I can't! O'Keefe is alive! He's too heavy for me to carry out of here on my own. I need you to come with me.'

The robot's face was incapable of expression, but the Doctor could sense its frustration. Someone was going to have a field day in the study of artificial emotions when this was over.

'+WAIT HERE.+'

Twelve clambered out of the pit, sections of metal plating sliding back from its abdomen revealing a range of specialist tools.

Blue flame spat from a concealed nozzle on its arm – a welding torch of some kind. The Doctor heard the click of servos and valves as the robot adjusted the gas mixture, and the neat blue flame suddenly transformed into a blazing sheet of smoky yellow fire.

The creatures were terrified.

They clawed their way backwards, shrieking horribly, pain making them shrill and loud. Twelve scooped up the limp and shattered body of the one it had killed. With a click and a hiss, a thin spray of viscous fluid sprayed over the limp shape and the Doctor smelled the sharp tang of oil. Twelve lifted the body and played the roaring flame over it.

The corpse erupted into a blazing ball of skin and fur. The Doctor had to shield his face from the heat. The robot hurled the burning mass into the cavern looking for all the world as if it was some bizarre ten-pin bowler, and the creatures scattered, vanishing down tunnels and fissures, desperate to escape the heat and flame.

Twelve stepped back into the pit, the flame shutting off, melting ice steaming on the robot's metal skin. There was a worryingly loud crack from the ice overhead. Effortlessly, the robot gathered the lolling body of Maxwell O'Keefe into its arms and turned to the Doctor with its expressionless face.

'+WE NEED TO LEAVE NOW.+'

The Doctor didn't need telling twice and scrambled up the chunks of melting ice to the huge ragged hole that the robot had forced through from the service corridor. Back in the cavern, the angry cries of the creatures started to get louder as the flames started to die.

Halfway along the fissure, Twelve placed O'Keefe on the ground and started to drag huge chunks of rock and ice from the walls, sealing the tunnel behind them. The Doctor watched with a heavy heart as the irreplaceable cave paintings that had brought so many people to their deaths in this icy cavern were consigned to the barricade, no more than a barrier now, giving them time to escape.

Another bellow of anger spurred them forward. Twelve had done a good job of blocking the tunnel, but the creatures were desperate and hungry, and very, very angry, and the Doctor wasn't sure that it was going to hold them for long.

Dim fluorescent light appeared ahead of them, and the Doctor gratefully climbed out of the fissure into the service corridor. He clutched at his side, taking in deep breaths. He was getting out of condition.

He dodged out of the way as Twelve lumbered out into the corridor after him.

'+I DID NOT HAVE TIME TO MAKE AN ADEQUATE BARRICADE. MY ESTIMATE IS THAT IT WILL ONLY BE THIRTY PER CENT EFFECTIVE.+'

'Well, no one's perfect.'

'+I WILL ATTEMPT TO CREATE A BARRIER AT THIS END OF THE FISSURE.+'

The big robot placed O'Keefe gingerly on the cold concrete floor and turned to the pile of abandoned equipment in the passageway.

The Doctor held up his hand. 'Hold on a minute, big guy. I think that some of this stuff might be more use than simply as barricade fodder.'

He peered at the tangle of tools and metal that was heaped in the corridor. 'Do you think you could get that free?' He pointed at the back end of an anti-grav sled that jutted out from the pile.

There was a shower of sparks and a grinding shriek of tortured metal as Twelve started clearing shattered equipment from on top of the sled.

The Doctor crouched next to O'Keefe's unconscious body as pieces of abandoned equipment were dragged from the accident site and hurled to one side. O'Keefe's breathing was fast and shallow, and he'd shown no sign of regaining consciousness as he had back in the cavern. The Doctor placed his hand on the man's forehead. His skin was clammy and grey and his eyelids constantly flickered. Whatever the process was that had affected the others, it had begun to happen to O'Keefe. The only hope he had was that they might get him back to the sickbay and find some kind of antidote.

The Doctor looked grimly at his patient. He had another reason for getting O'Keefe back to the infirmary. Contacting the adult creature's mind directly had proved too dangerous, the raw primal energy that it generated had been too much for him to cope with. But if he was right, if O'Keefe was infected, then an embryonic creature was slowly taking form inside him and maybe contact with that would give him the answers he needed.

The Doctor knew that he was playing with the man's life, and he hated himself for it, but at present Maxwell O'Keefe was the best hope he had of dealing with the creatures before they found their way into SnowGlobe 6 and turned it into a bloodbath. Perhaps the only hope.

The baying cries of the creatures made him look up in alarm. The noise was closer. The creatures had got through the barricade.

'Twelve, I think we're going to have company in a minute. How are you doing over there?'

With a grinding roar, the construction robot hauled the anti-grav sled free of the pile of wreckage, lifting it as though it was a toy and placing it down on the floor of the tunnel.

The Doctor leapt to his feet, hopping up onto the sled and brushing ice and debris from the controls. Several lights and readouts were smashed, and the steering column was buckled and twisted.

Crouching down, the Doctor opened up a small inspection plate, slipping on his glasses and peering into the workings of the machine.

'Not bad, Twelve, not bad at all. Most of the primary systems are still operational. Gyros are a bit wonky, though, so we won't have the smoothest of rides.'

There was another angry snarl from the fissure, much closer than before.

Twelve turned towards the tunnel mouth. '+FOUR LIFE SIGNS APPROACHING RAPIDLY. FIFTY-FIVE METRES AND CLOSING.+'

'Well don't just stand there,' snapped the Doctor. 'Get O'Keefe onto the sled.'

'+DAMAGE TO THE ANTI-GRAVITY DEVICE IS SEVERE. IT IS UNLIKELY THAT YOU WILL BE ABLE TO SUCCESSFULLY ACTIVATE IT. LIFE FORMS FORTY METRES AND CLOSING.+'

'Well, it's nice to see that I've got your complete confidence. Let me worry about the sled, just get O'Keefe and get on board.'

The robot lifted O'Keefe and placed him gently on the rear of the anti-grav sled, then clambered up alongside him, folding down onto one of the sled's long metal equipment racks.

The Doctor pulled frantically at wires and connections in the guts of the control panel. The drive systems were intact. If he could just get a charge to the starter circuit…

'Twelve, open your inspection hatch.'

There was a click and a small panel on the robot's chest sprang open.

'+THIRTY METRES.+'

The Doctor reached deep into the guts of the sled's controls and hauled out a long, finger-thick cable with a multi-pinned plug on the end.

The robot tilted a dispassionate head towards him. '+THE CONNECTORS FOR BAZ INDUSTRIES ANTI-GRAV SLEDS ARE NOT COMPATABLE WITH ANY OF MY SOCKETS OR HUBS. TWENTY METRES.+'

'Always the way with peripherals, isn't it? Never got the right adaptor. Ah well. I'll just have to hotwire it.'

The Doctor jammed the cable into Twelve's exposed circuitry and jabbed at his sonic screwdriver.

With a roar of power, the sled jumped into the air, almost sending the Doctor tumbling. Lights were blinking erratically across the damaged panel, and the power systems were wavering and whining alarmingly, but the sled was working.

'Oh ye of little faith!'

'+TEN METRES.+'

The Doctor grabbed hold of the twisted steering column

and pushed it hard. The sled shot forwards, in a flurry of snow and ice. The Doctor gave a whoop of triumph.

From behind them, he could hear angry hissing. He glanced over his shoulder to see the creatures tumble out into the corridor and start scuttling along the tunnel after them.

They weren't going to give up their prey so easily.

FIFTEEN

'**R**ight. We'd better get after Cowley.' Martha dropped the heavy bio-hazard suit into a disposal bin and shrugged on her jacket.

All the patients were back in what remained of their beds in the ward and heavily tranquillised.

Dr Jaffa and Harrison lay on the gurneys at the far end of the ward, eyes flickering wildly under their eyelids like all the others.

Ku'ra looked over at Martha. 'I'll come with you.'

'You sure? It could be dangerous.'

'As if the last couple of hours with you *haven't* been dangerous?'

'OK, fair point.' Martha grinned at him. 'Thanks. I could use the help.'

As they crossed to the door, one of the security guards stepped in front of them, blocking their way.

'Where do you think you two are going?'

'We told you. We've got to get after Director Cowley.'

'I'm sorry, Miss. I can't let you leave until I have instructions from Captain Hassan.'

'Weren't you listening just now?' snapped Ku'ra. 'The Director has got a case full of highly contagious biological material. If she gets out of the dome…'

'And I have told you that this dome is completely locked down. If Director Cowley poses some kind of threat, then she won't get far.'

'So start looking for her!' Martha was getting impatient.

'We will, Dr Jones, just as soon as I get instructions—'

'From Captain Hassan.' Martha shook her head. 'We don't have time for this.'

She tried to push past the guard. He grabbed hold of her arm, spinning her around. Martha shoved him hard, and he went stumbling backwards. She reached for the door controls then froze as she heard the harsh click of a machine gun being cocked.

Martha turned round slowly. The other guard, alerted by the sounds of struggle, was standing in the doorway of the ward, her gun pointed at Martha's head. She shook her head slowly. 'That was an extremely stupid thing to do, Dr Jones. Now please step away from—'

The guard broke off as her face suddenly went slack, and she sank slowly to the floor, gun dropping from her fingers. Marisha stood behind her, a tranquillising hypo in her hand. The other guard was struggling to his feet, reaching for his gun. Marisha crossed the room in three quick strides and pressed the hypo against his neck. With a groan, he collapsed in an untidy heap.

Martha gave a huge sigh of relief. 'Remind me never to get on the wrong side of you, girl!'

Marisha gave her a guilty smile. 'I don't like people waving guns around in my ward. Besides,' she nodded at the two unconscious guards. 'If Hassan has locked the place down, you're going to need these uniforms to get out.'

'I'm impressed.' Martha helped Marisha haul the male guard onto the sofa and started pulling off his jacket. 'Let's just hope they were right about Cowley not being able to get out, 'cos if she has then Dubai is an awfully large place to search.'

Beth Cowley clambered out of the ventilation shaft into a small, empty room and stood blinking in the afternoon sunlight that filtered in through the windows set high in the wall. She stood for a moment, her eyes adjusting after so long in the gloom of the tunnels.

She crossed the room, unlocking the double doors and stepping out into the fresh air. The shaft had emerged in a low cluster of maintenance buildings, set discreetly back from the beach, their low concrete shapes softened by small shrubs and tall date palms.

Cowley breathed in the fresh air, clearing her lungs of the dust and grime from the shaft. Slowly, she made her way down to the beachfront. People gave her curious looks as she meandered to the water's edge. She must have looked an odd sight, her suit streaked with grease and dirt, incongruous amongst the bathing costumes of the holidaymakers.

Cowley glared at the onlookers and they turned away, returning to their games and books, already dismissing her from their thoughts. She despised them. They didn't care about the past, didn't care about the work that she had tried to do, didn't care that the very fact of their constant need to jet off somewhere that was hot and comfortable and that catered for their every whim had brought the planet that they lived on to the very brink of destruction.

She closed her eyes, concentrating on the voice in her head, the voice that made her feel so calm and serene, the voice that had shown her how much better the future could be. She could sense the creatures far below, sense their rage and hunger. Something had angered them.

A smile flickered across her face.

The Doctor.

He had been so arrogant, assuming that he knew everything. It pleased her to think of him reduced to no more than a host for the creatures that she now served.

A breeze from the sea ruffled her hair, and she opened her eyes. A passenger shuttle swooped low over the sea, its engine droning, the noise carried landwards by the wind. Cowley craned her neck back as it circled overhead before settling onto the shuttle pad that jutted out from the top of the Burj Al-Arab hotel.

Calm and single-minded once more, Cowley nodded to herself. Yes. That was perfect. The sea breeze would ensure that the dust would be carried over the entire city. It was time for her to finish her task. She would release the dust from the case, and the planet would be cleansed.

No one on the beach gave her so much as a second

glance as she picked up the metal case and started along the shoreline.

The anti-grav sled raced down the service corridor. If there hadn't been half a dozen ravening monsters on their tail, the Doctor would have been enjoying himself. Every now and then, he checked the numbers on the walls against the blueprints on the pad that Roberts had given him, the little device perched precariously on the control column of the sled as if it were a sat-nav.

It had always been the Doctor's intention to use the service corridor to get back out of the dome. If he was right, the tunnel ran right alongside Roberts' maintenance workshop. It was one of the main reasons that he had brought Twelve along. Heavy-duty construction robots were handy things to have when you wanted a wall demolished.

The problem was he hadn't been intending to have an injured man in tow, and he certainly hadn't intended to be leading the creatures right to the very people he was hoping to save. Having now seen how the creatures reacted to flame, he was desperately hoping that Technician Roberts would have the equipment that he needed to construct a suitable deterrent.

Another sign flashed past, and the Doctor tried to match it to one of the identification markers on the screen in front of him. Good. They had nearly made it.

He almost didn't see the creature until it was too late. He just looked up and suddenly it was there, hanging from the pipes in the roof ahead of them like some malevolent bat.

The Doctor ducked as claws slashed down at him, wrenching the control column to one side. With a shriek of metal, the sled cannoned off a tangle of pipes on the tunnel wall, its engines screaming. He tried frantically to correct the course of the careering craft, but his makeshift repairs had been pushed to the limit.

With a horrible grinding of gears and a spurt of hot sparks from the exposed wiring, the sled slammed into a wall, sending the Doctor flying. He bounced painfully across the concrete floor, crashing into a pile of oil drums.

He struggled to his feet, desperately looking for the creature. In his urgency to get away from the swarm in the cavern, he had completely forgotten that one of them had made its way past him into the service corridor earlier. And he had driven right into it.

He looked back at the sled. O'Keefe was lolling awkwardly off the back. Twelve had been thrown off further down the corridor and was lying in an ungainly heap.

'Twelve, are you all right?' the Doctor asked.

The robot hauled itself upright.

'+MY MAJOR FUNCTIONS ARE UNIMPAIRED.+'

'Well get over here then, I'm going to need you.'

A low, sibilant hiss made him look up. The creature was untangling itself from amongst the pipes in the ceiling. Slowly, it lowered itself to the floor. The Doctor looked frantically around for something that he could use to defend himself.

The creature started to circle him, fingers flexing in anticipation. The Doctor pressed himself up against the tunnel wall, and gave a cry of pain as his hands touched something scalding hot.

The Doctor looked down. The impact had torn insulation from the thick metal pipes that ran down the tunnel. Further down the corridor he could see vapour jetting into the corridor from where the sled had crashed into the wall.

It was steam. Scalding hot steam.

'Twelve!' shouted the Doctor. 'The steam pipe – tear it off the wall. Quickly!'

The robot marched over to the damaged pipe and tore it effortlessly from the wall. Steam erupted into the corridor.

The effect on the creature was immediate and dramatic. Screaming in terror, it skittered away from the blast of vapour, curling its arms around its body, like a spider caught in a bathtub. Twelve wrenched the pipe free of its fixings and swung the hissing, spitting nozzle at the creature. There was a shriek of agony as the billowing white clouds enveloped it, then silence.

The Doctor darted over to a valve on the wall and twisted it to the off position. The roaring steam shut off abruptly, the pipes groaning and clicking noisily as they cooled.

Cautiously, the Doctor moved over to the motionless remains of the creature. It had curled into a twisted black lump, literally cooked in the steam. The Doctor rubbed his chin thoughtfully. It was obvious now that the creatures had little if any tolerance to heat. That was the best defence against them.

From a long way back down the corridor came a mournful, drawn-out wail of anger and rage. The Doctor could feel a tickle of telepathic energy. The creatures had sensed the death of one of their kind.

The Doctor patted Twelve on the arm. 'Come on. We're nearly there. Will you get Mr O'Keefe?'

Twelve nodded, scooped O'Keefe's body into its arms and set off down the corridor. With a last sad look at the steaming remains of the creature, the Doctor hurried after him.

Martha and Ku'ra hurried down the steps from the main administration building, caps pulled down tight on their heads, machine guns slung over their shoulders. All around them, tourists and holidaymakers were milling around in confusion. A few tried to stop them, anxious to find out what was going on, but Ku'ra glared at them and the tourists backed off hurriedly

The two of them made their way down towards the main airlock, Ku'ra's stern expression (and the two guns) keeping the curious at bay. The entire dome had a vague, uneasy feel. The tourists seemed to be aware that something was wrong, but Martha knew that none of them understood the true nature of the danger facing them. As they reached the main doors, she saw the reason for the tourists' unease: armed guards formed a solid line across the exits, dozens of military vehicles visible through the glass of the dome.

'Cowley's never going to have made it out past that lot.' Ku'ra nodded towards the troops.

'I'm not so sure.' Martha chewed at her lip. 'She's the

Director of the SnowGlobe, remember? And you saw how she was with Jaffa. Would *you* try to stop her?'

'OK. Point taken. So how do *we* get out?'

'Dressed like this, I'm hoping we just march out.'

'Just like that?'

'Trick of the Doctor's. Act as though you own the place. Come on, Private Debrekseny.'

'Yes, ma'am.' Ku'ra gave her a sharp salute and the two of them started towards the doors.

As they drew closer, Martha caught sight of a familiar figure on one of the gantries. 'Keep your head down,' she whispered. 'Hassan's on the walkway to our left.'

Ku'ra pulled his cap down low over his eyes, keeping a steady gaze on the doorway ahead of them. They joined a line of soldiers making their way out through a service hatchway, armed guards checking their nametags as they filed through.

'This could get tricky if they ask any awkward questions,' muttered Ku'ra.

Martha crossed her fingers, wishing, not for the first time, that the Doctor had left her his psychic paper. The sergeant on the gate waved them forward, and Martha and Ku'ra marched over to the security point.

He waved what looked like a barcode reader over the nametags on the breast pockets of their jackets, scrutinising a small screen set into his desk.

He grunted. 'You're from Hassan's team, aren't you? You know you've not got exit clearance at this time. Shift change isn't for another two hours.'

Martha froze, her brain racing.

Ku'ra snapped to attention. 'Captain Hassan requested that we report to him directly outside the dome following our security sweep, sir.'

'Really, Private?' The sergeant stood up, staring straight into Ku'ra's face.

Martha's heart leapt into her mouth. With Hassan standing barely four metres away, all the sergeant had to do was check and their deception would be blown wide open.

'Sergeant.' Hassan's voice rang out across the tarmac. 'Are those the two of my security personnel that I asked to do a sweep of the medical wing?'

'Yes, sir!' the sergeant bellowed.

'Good. Send them through to my command post. I'll debrief them there.'

'Very good, sir.' The sergeant saluted, then scowled at Ku'ra and Martha. 'All right, you two. Through you go. And quick about it.'

Ku'ra marched though the doorway. Martha hurried after him, unable to believe her luck.

As they stepped through into the blazing afternoon sun, she stared at him in astonishment. 'How on earth…?'

'Promise you'll not get mad at me?'

'Of course not!'

Ku'ra tapped the side of his head. 'Did what I'm not supposed to. Reached into Hassan's mind. Realised what he was going to say and got there first.'

Martha wanted to hug him. Instead she caught hold of his arm and dragged him around the side of the dome, heading away from the troops and security personnel milling around in the car park and towards the beach. As soon as they were out of view of the entrance, the two of them shrugged out of their borrowed uniforms, bundled the rifles inside them and buried them under a cluster of Eucalyptus bushes.

'OK, mister,' Martha said, sitting Ku'ra down. 'You've convinced me that your gift is very useful, and I don't see any other way of tracking down Cowley, do you?'

Ku'ra frowned. 'Plucking a thought from someone who's practically standing next to me is a far cry from finding one individual in an entire city.'

'An individual whose mind is probably different from everyone else's. That's gotta help, right?'

'OK.' Ku'ra shrugged. 'I'll give it a try.'

'You'd better do more than try, Ku'ra.' Martha stared at the thousands of people scattered across the beach. 'If this doesn't work, we're never going to find her.'

Rabley lowered himself slowly into the debris of the corridor, unable to believe that he was still alive.

When the creature had first appeared in the mouth of the ventilation shaft, Rabley had had a moment of complete and utter terror. Frozen with fear, he had only been able to watch as the thing had inched its way slowly forwards, its long fingers feeling and searching, its echo-location pinging around the confined space.

Rabley had backed himself tight against one of the huge whirring fans, whimpering, fumbling vainly for the gun hidden in the waistband of his trousers and realising with despair that he no longer had it.

Then the creature's probing fingers had caught hold of the bag containing the money and something had snapped in him. It was his money, and he was damned if he was going to let some oversized spider from another planet take it away from him. He had clawed back the bag, shouting and kicking and screaming at the creature. Taken by surprise, the creature had relinquished its grip on the holdall, recoiling backwards into the confined mouth of the ventilation shaft.

That moment of hesitation had been all that Rabley had needed. He had snatched up anything that wasn't bolted down, hurling lengths of pipe, spanners, wrenches down the shaft, screaming and shouting at the top of his voice. Rabley had had no idea if any of his impromptu missiles had actually hit the creature, but the noise, surprise and confusion had been enough to drive it away.

He had sat in the cramped space of the fan room for a while, clutching the bag, listening for signs of the creature. Then he'd started to laugh, nervously at first, but soon with great, whooping guffaws. He was alive!

Gradually his laughter had subsided, and he had peered cautiously down the shaft. He had heard the clicking from its echo-location somewhere below him and darting shadows moved at the bottom of the shaft. After a time, his elation at having beaten off the monster had turned to panic once more. There was no way out of the fan room and the only way to climb down the shaft was to go backwards. If the creature decided to attack, he would have no chance whatsoever. On top of that, he had no food or water. If it wanted to, the creature could just wait until he was too weak to fight and then come and get him at its leisure.

He had been sitting there pondering his options when there had been a splintering crash from below. The walls of the fan room had shaken with the force of the impact and, with a spluttering of sparks and a whine of protesting motors, the fans had shut down and the lights had gone out.

Rabley had sat in the dark, wondering if the creatures had the intelligence to shut off the power themselves. Slowly though he had realised that something else was going on in the tunnel below. He heard hissing and grinding metal, raised voices and the high shrill cries of the creature.

Realising the creature had found something else to distract it and this might be his only chance at escape, he had hurried down the shaft, dragging the holdall after him. He had climbed as quickly as he dared, feet slipping on the greasy rungs of the ladder as he scrambled back down towards the service corridor.

As he had reached the bottom of the shaft, a huge cloud of steam had billowed upwards, half-blinding him. For a moment he had thought that he was going to lose his grip and plummet into the corridor below, but the scalding steam had abruptly dissipated, and there had been silence,

Rabley had hung there, just inside the hatchway, listening. A huge shape had passed underneath him. A service robot of some kind? There was a man's voice. He had strained to hear, desperate to know what was going on below, but the words that he heard had almost made his heart stop.

'Come on. We're nearly there. Will you get Mr O'Keefe?'

Moments later, the robot had clumped underneath the hatchway again, a limp form in its arms. Rabley had needed no second look to know who the robot was carrying: the size and shape of the man had been unmistakable.

As the footsteps had faded into silence, Rabley had squeezed himself out of the hatchway and lowered himself slowly to the floor.

Now he was standing amongst the wreckage in the corridor. The holdall over his shoulder and the money it contained suddenly felt very heavy indeed.

He shook his head very slowly. How could O'Keefe possibly still be alive? He had seen the creatures hunt him down. It was impossible that his employer had been able to outrun them.

He suddenly felt sick. O'Keefe was alive, and that meant that his entire plan was worth nothing. No chance of vanishing with the money, no chance of convincing people that he had perished in the dome, no chance that Bunta and his trained thugs wouldn't guess exactly what he had been planning.

Rabley slumped down on his haunches. That house in Ireland had been so close. His only chance now was to try and get back inside SnowGlobe 6, put the money *back* in the safe and try and convince O'Keefe that he had been planning to go for help all along.

He chewed his fingernails nervously. It shouldn't be *too* difficult to make up some story that sounded convincing. With luck, he would be able to pick up where he left off.

No one would ever be any the wiser.

A long, drawn-out howl from further along the corridor made his blood freeze. The creatures were out of the dome and they were heading his way!

Grabbing the holdall, Curtis Rabley turned and fled.

SIXTEEN

Technician Roberts was just settling down with a nice cup of tea brewed on one of the workshop's Bunsen burners, when his mobile gave a shrill warbling trill. He snatched it up in irritation, peering at the number on the screen. It was the communicator he had given the Doctor. He answered the call, wincing as a cacophony of noise blared through the headset. 'Doctor? What the devil is all that noise?'

'Mr Roberts!' The Doctor sounded breathless. 'No time to chat right now, I'm afraid. Are you on your own at the moment?'

'Yes. Why?'

'And are you anywhere near the far wall, the one that runs at right angles to the robot storage bay?'

'No, I'm in my office. Why on earth—'

'Good-oh. See you in a second.'

The phone went dead. Moments later there was a tremendous crash, and the wall on the far side of the workshop exploded inwards in a cloud of dust and masonry. Roberts stared in astonishment as Service Robot Twelve stepped through the ragged hole, a limp body in its arms. The Doctor scrambled after it, coughing and spluttering.

Roberts pushed open his office door and stepped out into the wreckage of his workshop, his face like thunder.

'I don't believe it! What the devil are you playing at, man?'

The Doctor bounded across to him, catching him by the shoulders. 'Mr Roberts, I will explain everything to you, I promise, but right now I've got half a dozen very angry predators on my tail, and we need to work fast to stop them getting into the dome. So do you have any high-pressure steam or high-energy heating equipment that we can use to create a barrier?'

Roberts gaped at him. 'You mean that those things are—'

'Mr Roberts. The only thing that can stop these creatures is heat, but we need to work very, very, very fast!'

Roberts took a deep breath. 'All right. We've got plasma heaters. We used them at low levels for the work teams when we were building the place, but if we override the safety cut-outs—'

'Do it.'

Roberts hurried over to where the robots stood motionless in their cradles, stabbing at buttons. Six metal heads swung down in unison.

'+READY TO RECEIVE COMMANDS.+'

'OK, you lot,' bellowed Roberts. 'Break out the R-7

heater units. Get them over to me for calibration and then get them out into the service corridor. Move it!' The workshop was filled with the sound of motors and hydraulics whining into life as the robots stepped down from their alcoves and started unpacking huge cylindrical shapes from a rack on the far side of the workshop. Roberts darted between them as the cylinders were lowered to the floor, tapping at a series of controls set into the cylinders' sides.

One of the robots swung a metal face towards him.

'+TECHNICIAN ROBERTS. YOUR CALIBRATIONS ARE PUTTING THESE MACHINES OUTSIDE OF THEIR RECOMMENDED SAFETY PARAMETERS.+'

'And if I want any advice from you then I'll ask for it. Now just get on with what you've been told.'

'+YES, TECHNICIAN ROBERTS.+'

Roberts rolled his eyes at the Doctor. 'Everyone's an expert suddenly.'

'These heaters will do the job?' the Doctor asked.

'These things can melt steel if you don't treat 'em properly. If your beasties don't like the heat, they should get quite a shock.'

'Good. If we can just create a barricade long enough for me to get some answers.'

Roberts looked quizzically at the limp body hanging in Twelve's arms.

'Isn't that Maxwell O'Keefe?'

'The same.'

'Is he all right?'

'No.' The Doctor placed a hand on O'Keefe's forehead.

'He's a very long way from all right.' He straightened, his face grim. 'Mr Roberts, I've got to get O'Keefe up to the medical bay. Will you be all right here?'

'Sure.' Roberts paled slightly. 'As long as you're right about those thingies and their aversion to heat.'

The Doctor clapped him on the shoulder. 'You and your boys hold the fort here. I'll be back as soon as I can. Come on, Twelve!' With that, he swept out of the room.

Roberts watched him go, then turned to face the gaping hole in the workshop wall. 'You'd better be right, Doctor. You'd better be right.'

Cowley craned her neck back and stared up at the slim, elegant tower of the Burj Al-Arab hotel. It would suit her purposes admirably.

She stepped through into the huge spacious atrium, goosebumps rising on her skin as the cool, air-conditioned air of the lobby replaced the heat of the afternoon sun. A service robot glided over to her, metal arms reaching for the metal case that she clutched to her chest.

'+MAY I TAKE THAT FOR YOU, MA'AM?+'

Cowley hesitated for a moment, unhappy to relinquish her prize, when a sudden thought struck her. She slipped a small, silver strip from her jacket pocket. Her company credit stick. Why should she go to all the trouble of trying to make her way to the top of the hotel surreptitiously? She could pay for the best suite in the place and let the robot carry the case for her. It wasn't as if anyone was ever going to chase her for the money. Not after she had completed her task at any rate.

Smiling to herself, she let the robot take the case, following it over to the gleaming reception desk. A slim, young man looked up expectantly.

'Good afternoon. Can I help?'

'I'd like a room please. The top floor if possible.'

The young man checked a screen on his desk. 'A penthouse suite *is* currently available. Will it just be yourself?'

Cowley nodded.

'And how will you be paying?' The man raised an expectant eyebrow.

Cowley handed over the credit stick. A look of surprise crossed the receptionist's face as he fed the stick into the reader. 'Director Cowley? This is a pleasant surprise. Your SnowGlobes have been quite a boon to our hotel over the years. A special occasion is it?'

'Something like that.'

'Well, I'm sure that we can arrange some kind of discount for you…'

'That would be very kind. Now, if you don't mind, I'm rather tired.'

'Of course.'

The receptionist tapped a series of commands into his keyboard. The service robot carrying the case turned and glided across the lobby. 'If you would follow the robot it will show you to your suite, Director.' He handed her back her credit stick and a key card. 'If there's anything you need, please don't hesitate to call.'

'Thank you.' Cowley took the proffered card and followed the robot to one of the waiting lifts.

The doors slid shut, and the lift started its climb towards the top of the hotel. The receptionist had been right. This was a special occasion. A night when she would change the face of the planet for ever.

Marisha was slowly starting the process of getting the medical bay back into some semblance of normality when the Doctor burst into the reception area. Her smile of relief at seeing him faded as the shape of a huge service robot squeezed through the doors behind him.

'Got a patient for you, nurse.' The Doctor smiled apologetically.

Marisha hurried forward. The man in the robot's arms was in a bad way, his skin pale to the point of transparency, his breathing shallow and rapid. Marisha gasped as readings started to scroll across the screen of her medical scanner.

'This man. He's—'

'A host. Yes, I know.' The Doctor took the scanner off her, peering at the screen. 'We've not got much time left. I need you to help me set up a neurological feedback integrator.'

Marisha looked at him blankly. 'A what?'

'Look, I'll explain as we work,' said the Doctor impatiently. 'Where can we put him?'

'He can't go in with the others. We'll have put him into the morgue.'

Marisha hurried over to the big steel door, hauling it open. Twelve stomped over, ducking to get through the doorway. The Doctor frowned as he slowly started to take in the state of the room. 'Have you been having some problems?'

Marisha gave a snort of amusement. 'You could say that. Our patients decided to get a little… animated. It got a bit frantic in here for a while.'

'Ah… The influence of our hairy friend in the other dome no doubt.' The Doctor looked around, concerned. 'Where's Martha?'

Marisha sighed. 'You're not going to like this.'

As they made O'Keefe as comfortable as they could on the metal examination table, Marisha explained to the Doctor what had gone on over the last hour or so: the mental signal that had turned the patients into rabid zombies; Cowley escaping with the eggs; Martha's attempt to escape; drugging the guards.

The Doctor listened in silence, but Marisha could see from the tense line of his jaw that he wasn't happy. When she had finished, he just stared at O'Keefe's body, suddenly looking so much older.

Marisha touched his arm, 'Hey, she'll be all right.'

'Yes, she will.' The Doctor's voice was cold.

He pulled a slim, metal tube from his jacket pocket, snatched Marisha's diagnostic pad from her hands and started to dismantle it. Before Marisha could complain, he vanished into the ward, reappearing a few moments later with armfuls of equipment.

'What on earth are you doing?' she asked.

'Here, hold this.' The Doctor dumped a plastic tray piled high with components into her arms. Squatting down cross-legged on the floor, the Doctor started to wire components together. To Marisha, it looked like a total lash up, but the Doctor worked quickly and methodically, finally sitting back with a cry of triumph.

'That should do it!'

'Do what?' Marisha stared at the jumble of equipment. Wires snaked everywhere – he seemed to have connected up almost every piece of equipment in the ward. One thick cable terminated in a series of sensors that the Doctor had attached to O'Keefe's skull; another led to a collection of headsets and earpieces that the Doctor had welded together to form a bizarre helmet.

'The creatures have a complex mental communication system,' he explained. 'They use it to communicate with each other, and to draw in their prey. I'd hoped to use my own telepathic ability to communicate directly with them, but the frequencies they use are too strong, too primal.' The Doctor wedged the helmet onto his head, tying a strap under his chin. 'I'm hoping that the embryonic form of the creature inside Mr O'Keefe here will still be in contact with the parent creature…'

'But with a reduced mental ability.'

'Exactly! So I intend to access the parent creature's mind through the brain of its offspring.'

Marisha grimaced. 'So this device is going to allow you to link your mind with the thing inside him?'

'Yes.'

'Isn't that potentially dangerous?'

'Oh yes.'

'But why? What do you hope to find out?'

'The parent creature has been in the ice since the last Ice

Age. If I can access its memory, I can find out how it got there, how it got to Earth in the first place.'

'How to destroy them?'

'If it comes to that, yes.'

Marisha nodded. 'What do you want me to do?'

'Keep O'Keefe sedated. Monitor my brainwave activity on this.' The Doctor handed Marisha the diagnostic pad. He had connected it to his tangle of machinery with bundles of twisted cables. Two undulating lines scrolled across the screen. 'Make sure that my brainwave patterns stay separate from those of the creature.'

'And if they start to merge?'

'It will mean that I've totally misunderstood how the creature's mental ability works, and I could be trapped in its mind for ever.'

Marisha swallowed hard. 'So I should unplug you before you reach that point?'

'If you wouldn't mind.' The Doctor shot her a weak smile. 'Wish me luck.'

He plugged himself into the machine.

SEVENTEEN

Martha paced nervously along the beachfront, squinting as the sun started to drop towards the horizon, the palm trees starting to cast long shadows across the white sand. Ku'ra was sitting up against one of those palm trees, eyes closed, fingers pressed to his temples. He had been like this for what seemed an age. The waiting was driving Martha crazy.

Ku'ra had explained to her that his mixed parentage had given him a disadvantage from his fellow Flisk – at least when it came to his telepathic ability. It did, however, give him a better understanding of the human mind. That, and the fact that Cowley's thoughts were tainted with those of the creatures, might make her mind easier to spot amongst the thousands that thronged the seafront.

He had dropped himself into a kind of trace, something that the Flisk called 'Ple'nsagh'. It obviously held some ritual or religious significance, and Ku'ra had been uncomfortable talking to Martha about it. Unable to do anything useful, she had left him to it, praying that this gamble would work.

She ambled down to the sea, closing her eyes and basking in the warmth of the setting sun for a moment. Out here on the beach, surrounded by happy, contented people, it seemed inconceivable that a struggle for the lives of every creature on the planet was taking place.

She squatted down on her haunches, scooping up a handful of sand and letting it run through her fingers. The smell of the sea was carried in on the wind.

A sudden thought struck her. She snatched up another handful of the dry, white sand and let it run out in a stream through her fist, watching the wind whisk the grains up the beach. The case that Cowley was carrying must be pure dust by now. If she was going to release it over the populace, she would have to rely on the wind to carry it.

She scrambled to her feet, her mind racing. The wind was blowing in from the sea, so Cowley would probably have stayed by the coast. But where?

A long, slim shadow slicing across the beach caught Martha's eye. Slowly she followed the streak of shadow to the tall, elegant tower in the bay. From behind her, she could hear someone shouting her name.

Ku'ra skidded to a stop next to her, breathless and excited.

'Martha! I know where she is! I've found her.'

The two of them turned in unison and stared up at the Burj Al-Arab hotel silhouetted against the reddening sky.

Martha caught hold of Ku'ra's hand. 'Come on!'

***

Pain.

White light.

Then silence and darkness.

The Doctor is somewhere else.

Except he is not the Doctor any more. Not just the Doctor at any rate.

He looks down at the unfamiliar body. Black fur and long sinuous arms.

The world around is a twilight one of trees and creepers, frosted and barren, snow crystallising on jagged rocks and scrubby plants. The sky overhead is an unfamiliar green, shot through with streaks of purple. The crescents of six moons are visible through scudding clouds.

This is home.

His feet claw at the frozen mud. Around him, the children of seven generations mewl and spit. In his head he can feel the minds of the matriarchs of the rival territories.

The young are hungry. Food is scarce. The fighting has already begun. Like turn upon like. Blood flows. They will not survive to another birthing.

The Doctor feels the hunger in his own belly, the hunger from a dozen other minds close by. No. Two dozen. A hundred. A hundred thousand. A planet of predators.

But no more prey.

He centres his mind, separating Time Lord from Gappa.

Gappa. The creatures call themselves the Gappa.

Wrenching his mind free from the base primal urges of the creature, the Doctor studies the sky. This memory is from times long past. He recognises the patterns of the stars. These constellations are from a younger universe.

The vision changes as memories blur and flow into each other. A blizzard. The drifting snow covers body upon body, limbs stiff and lifeless. The young are dead. The planet is dead.

The Doctor cries out with the pain in his belly. Hunger is all-consuming.

The minds he can feel are all weak. Dying. Soon he will be the last.

Memories blur again.

He is fighting, struggling against the nets and ropes and blazing fingers of energy that dance and flare around him.

The part of him that is Gappa spits and shrieks in fury. The part that is still Doctor watches as the astronauts put their plan into effect. The force fields are designed to capture not kill. Their aim is to preserve, just as the humans in the dome are seeking to preserve the ice.

Human?

No. The humans at this time are barely up on their hind legs.

Humanoid certainly. A race of starfarers who have seen a world in peril and have come to save what they can. The Doctor smiles, approving. The universe is not all about killing and conquest, war and death.

He is somewhere else now, a dark place of metal and sharp angles. A spaceship. In flight. The Doctor can feel the vibration through the hull.

He frowns. Something in that vibration is not right. Something is wrong.

He flexes against the energy field that holds him. He has to warn them.

Too late.

Fire.

The Doctor feels the pain as the heat becomes too much. The ship is tumbling, falling. A small blue planet is filling the view through the windows.

Mercifully, the pain is gone. He has snow beneath his feet once more. The ship is a blazing wreck. He retreats from the flame. There are minds here, primitive like the food of home. Dull, slow, easy to manipulate.

The Doctor looks down at claws stained red with blood. The ache in his belly has gone. Bodies lie at his feet. When his strength has returned, the bodies will be hosts. A new hive on a new world.

Pain. Noise. Light.

Primitive their minds might be, but the inhabitants of this world have mastered fire.

The Doctor catches the scent of unwashed bodies and unwashed furs. He sees the anger and fear in the faces of the figures that surround him. The Gappa backs away snarling, but the Doctor recognises the humans that will be. Homo sapiens.

They slash at him with burning torches, driving him back, deeper and deeper into the cave. Rock gives way to ice. The tunnel is getting narrower and narrower.

He snarls and lashes at his tormentors. Flame burns his skin.

Abruptly, the world becomes a cacophony of falling ice. Then darkness. And nothingness.

The ice cocoons him. He sleeps.

The Gappa will survive in the ice. The Gappa will be reborn.

The Gappa.

The Gappa.

Roberts looked tentatively out through the shattered hole in the workshop wall to the service corridor beyond. He had to shield his face from the heat; the R-7 units were working better than expected. It was like an oven out there.

He craned his neck, trying to see if any of the creatures were still lurking beyond the heat haze. They had only just managed to get the last heater unit in place before the hunting pack had arrived; a boiling mass of fur and teeth sweeping down the corridor like an angry tide. Thank God the Doctor had been right about their aversion to high temperatures. The wall of heat sent out by the R-7s had stopped them dead in their tracks. The noise out there had been incredible.

That had been ten or twelve minutes ago, and most of the creatures – including the big one – had retreated back down the corridor, probably returning to their frozen lair in SnowGlobe 7. Now the only noise was the occasional distant hiss as one of the younger creatures ventured back along the corridor again, screaming its frustration at the barrier that was keeping it from its prey. Roberts could see its shadowy, spider-like shape through the shimmering haze of heat.

He pulled a grimy rag from his overalls and mopped the beads of sweat from his brow. Looked like they'd be safe as long as the power held. With the modifications that he'd made to the safety cut-outs, the heaters were drawing a lot of power. Roberts stuffed the rag back into his pocket. The more that he thought about it, the more he thought that he should check the power relays. At the very least he could ensure that he was ready to shut off all non-essential power to the rest of the dome if the need arose.

He was making his way over to the power room when the door to the workshop was pushed open by two of Hassan's security guards. Roberts groaned and hurried over to them, hoping that he could convince them that he was in no need of their help. Given that one of them was already looking in astonishment at the ragged hole in the wall, that was beginning to seem unlikely.

The high-pitched, frustrated scream of the creature in the corridor put paid to any chance of explanation.

The two guards scurried over to the hole, unshouldering their rifles. One of them peered tentatively through, then, with a cry of astonishment, unleashed a barrage of shots.

Roberts clamped his hands over his ears as automatic gunfire shook the room. As he watched, the second guard unhooked a grenade from his belt.

'NO! You'll damage the heating units!' Roberts bellowed, but it was too late.

There was a dull crump. The doors to the power room blew open in a shower of sparks. Lights flickered and there was a terrifying scream of triumph from the creature in the corridor.

Roberts could hear one of the guards screaming in agony, and then gunfire deafened him once more.

Rabley ducked, cowering behind a workbench as a second explosion rattled the workshop. He cursed his luck. Surely he wasn't going to have survived all this time only to be blown apart by some over-zealous security guard?

He had followed the man and the robot that was carrying Mr O'Keefe back along the corridor, conscious of the cries of the creature getting ever closer behind him. He had seen the man talking into a mobile of some kind, but had been unable to make out what was being said. Presumably he was arranging medical help of some kind.

When the big robot had placed O'Keefe on the floor and smashed its way through the tunnel wall, Rabley had scarcely believed his eyes. As escape plans went, it had been impressive. This mysterious stranger certainly didn't do anything the subtle way.

The robot had scooped up O'Keefe and vanished through the hole. Rabley had followed them, peering through into the room beyond. A workshop of some kind. Probably one of the maintenance levels. Checking that no one was looking his way, Rabley had scurried inside, ducking behind one of the workbenches.

There he had stayed, listening to the Doctor and the robot leave, watching the robots move heater after heater into the corridor, waiting for the moment when the technician was sufficiently distracted to make his escape.

That distraction had finally come, though Rabley now wished that it had been a distraction of a less explosive kind. He peered over the top of the workbench. Smoke was billowing from the hole in the workshop wall, a security guard firing blindly into the chaos. The technician, Roberts, was desperately trying to put out a fire that raged inside a fuse box of some kind. It was now or never.

Rabley hurried towards the door, stopping only to snatch up an aerosol can from a workbench, a plan forming in his head. Things were dropping right into his lap.

With a last glance back into the smoke-filled workshop,

Rabley vanished through the door.

Martha and Ku'ra burst into the lobby of the hotel, startling several guests who looked at them in distaste.

Martha gaped at the vast atrium. 'It's huge! We'll never find her.'

'Hang about.' Ku'ra sprinted over to the reception desk. Martha craned her neck back. The hotel was beautiful, a huge tower of gleaming marble and glass that seemed to go up for ever. Glass lifts glided up the walls, robots piled high with bags and suitcases slid silently across the polished floor.

'Martha! Come on!' Ku'ra was holding a set of lift doors open, much to the annoyance of an elderly couple who were waiting to go up to their room.

Martha hurried over to him. 'You've found her?'

Ku'ra grinned and help up a piece of paper with a room number written on it. 'Penthouse suite. Top floor.'

'She booked in?' Martha was incredulous.

Ku'ra shrugged. 'Can you think of a better way to get into a hotel unchallenged?'

Ignoring the tutting of the couple behind them, Martha gave Ku'ra a quick hug as the lift whisked them towards the top of the hotel.

The elderly couple got off on the twelfth floor, shooting Martha a dirty look as they left. She stuck her tongue out at them as the door closed.

Ku'ra gave her a nervous smile. 'Have you got any idea what we actually do we when finally catch up with Cowley?' he asked.

Martha grimaced. 'I was wondering when you were going to ask me that.'

'I'll take that as a "no", then.'

Martha tried to think what the Doctor would do. 'Let's busk it, shall we?'

The lift came to a halt at the top floor, and the doors slid open. Ku'ra and Martha stepped out into a plush, elegant corridor. There was a single set of double doors at the far end. Paying for the penthouse room obviously got you your privacy.

The two of them hurried down the corridor. One of the doors was open. Martha could feel a breeze blowing through the gap. Cautiously, they eased the door open, peering into the room beyond. The penthouse was huge and opulent. Of Director Cowley there was no sign.

Martha slipped through the gap, Ku'ra right behind her. Slowly they crept forward.

'Where is she?' hissed Martha.

Ku'ra indicated the picture window on the far side of the room. The window was open, thick curtains billowing in the wind. They hurried over. A wide balcony dotted with chairs and loungers swept across the entire frontage of the Penthouse suite. There was still no sign of Cowley.

'This is crazy.' Martha was beginning to worry. 'She can't just have vanished.'

Ku'ra stepped out onto the balcony and quickly beckoned for Martha to join him. At the seaward end of the balcony, a winding staircase led up to the rooftop landing pad. Obviously the very uppermost rooms catered for those guests with private helicopters or shuttles. With a brief glance at the dizzying view below, Martha followed Ku'ra up the staircase.

They stepped out onto a vast, flat expanse of metal. This high up, and out of the shelter of the hotel, the wind plucked at their clothes and hair, and Martha struggled to keep her footing. Ku'ra gripped her arm. Martha was about to thank him for his assistance when she realised that his grip wasn't meant to steady her, but to alert her to the figure that was standing on the shuttle pad with them.

Ten metres away, staring out over the city of Dubai and the deserts beyond, stood Beth Cowley, the case with its deadly contents at her feet. She had her back to them, seemingly oblivious to their presence. Ku'ra started moving towards her along one edge of the pad, indicating that Martha should head along the other side. The two of them crept forward. Martha wincing at every squeak that her shoes made on the metal, desperately hoping that the sound of the wind would mask the noise of their approach. She couldn't take her eyes from the case, so close to the edge of the pad.

They were within two metres of her when Cowley turned around.

For a moment the Director looked shocked, then a smile spread slowly across her face.

'Yes. Yes it's right that there should be witnesses.' Cowley's voice was slurred and dreamy. 'Someone will need to record this moment in history, the moment where the preservation of a new species took precedence over everything else.'

Ku'ra started to edge towards her, hands outstretched.

'We'll record whatever you like, Director, just give me the case.'

'The case?' Cowley frowned. 'No, the case is my legacy, my gift.' She scooped it up in her arms. 'Don't you understand? This is how the world will remember me.'

Martha sucked in a breath as Cowley took a step backwards towards the edge of the shuttle pad. She waved at Ku'ra to back off.

'Director Cowley.' Martha kept her voice low and calm. 'Beth. We know that you have been under a lot of strain. We also know that the creatures in the dome are able to affect people, to influence them, make them do things that they don't want to do.'

A frown creased Cowley's brow. Martha took a step closer. Was she getting through? 'Do you remember the Doctor, my friend? The Doctor is trying to communicate with the creatures. To find out what they want.'

'But I know what they want!' Cowley spat the words. 'I know! I don't need any "Doctor" to tell me.' Cowley tipped her head to one side, half-closing her eyes. 'They show me so many things.' Martha could see Ku'ra tensing himself to grab her.

'And what *do* they want?'

'The same thing as any other creature of course. To live. To survive. To breed and grow. She has been so alone in the ice. So alone. The last of her kind. This…' Cowley stroked the metal of the case. 'This is their lifeline. Their chance to start again. I can help them start again.'

She pushed with her thumb, and one of the catches on the case snapped open with a metallic click. Martha tried to keep the panic from her voice, watching from the corner of her eye as Ku'ra crept closer and closer.

'Beth! Director! You can't really want to do this. Think of the thousands, the millions of people who will die if you open that case. Human beings. Think of what you're about to do, please!'

'You think that I don't know what I'm doing?' Cowley pointed at the packed beach far below them. 'The humans that you are so concerned about, the thousands out there, simply don't care about this planet any more. They don't deserve to survive! They pretend to care, but when it comes down to it they cannot even be bothered to help save themselves. The creature in the dome has survived millennia, crossed countless light years of void. It survived in MY dome because of MY work. It deserves this planet more than we do.' She reached for the second clasp.

'Beth listen to me!' screamed Martha. The creature is influencing your mind.'

'You think that I haven't thought through the consequences of my actions?' Cowley looked at her pityingly, and at that moment Martha knew that they were too late to stop her. 'I know exactly what I am doing.'

Time slowed to a crawl. Ku'ra launched himself forward, just as Cowley snapped open the clasp. For a second, Martha thought that he would reach her in time, but she turned at the last moment, twisting away from him as he reached out for her. Ku'ra landed hard on his belly, only just stopping himself from plummeting over the edge of the shuttle pad. Cowley was not so lucky. One of her heels caught on the metal gratings. She started to topple.

With the heavy case in her arms she had no chance of regaining her balance. A gust of wind caught the lid of the case, flipping it open. Martha watched in horror as Cowley vanished over the edge, swathed in a cloud of billowing dust.

EIGHTEEN

'Doctor?' Marisha knelt down next to where the Doctor lay flat out on the office couch. He was pale, his lips blue, his fingers curled like claws.

'The Gappa. The Gappa…' His voice was harsh and low.

Marisha reached out and touched his shoulder tentatively. She leapt back with a cry as he sat bolt upright, eyes wide.

'Gappa! Gappa! Gappa! That was weird! And icky! And informative!'

He bounced to his feet, twirling Marisha around. He seemed to be practically fizzing with energy. 'Very old, very primitive, and all the way from Hydropellica Hydroxi, right on the far side of the Milky Way. Hermaphrodites, brutally powerful telepathic ability, strong aversion to heat and dreadfully itchy fur!'

He snatched the diagnostic pad from her. 'Did the lines merge?'

'They got close.'

'Not surprised! Amazingly strong race memory. Could have been in there for hours!'

'Doctor…' Marisha tailed off. The Doctor turned to look at her. 'You *were* in there for hours.'

The Doctor's jaw dropped. 'WHAT?'

A young, grim-faced security guard led the Doctor and Marisha out of the medical bay and down the corridor to the office that had been Director Cowley's. The ward that had once been filled with patients now housed only three. As they had passed through, the Doctor had watched with mounting concern as military personnel in bio-suits loaded one of those remaining three patients into a low, metal cryogenic capsule.

The guard pushed open the door of Cowley's office and ushered them through.

Inside, Hassan sat behind the desk, his face an unreadable mask. He indicated for the Doctor and Marisha to sit down.

'So, Doctor,' he said. 'You're quite the escape artist it seems.'

The Doctor grinned. 'I try my best, Captain. I try my best. Where is Mr O'Keefe?'

'She's not told you?' Hassan raised an eyebrow at Marisha.

'If she had told me, I wouldn't be asking.' The Doctor's grin faded.

'Tell him,' said Hassan.

'Whilst you were… in there, he had a seizure.' Marisha's

voice was trembling. 'I tried to resuscitate him but the thing started to move inside him… I… I couldn't save him.'

The Doctor laid a comforting hand on her shoulder. 'There was nothing that you, or any of us, could do for him. The creature, the Gappa, is too well established in his system.'

'And you knew that before you brought him back here?' asked Hassan.

The Doctor nodded. 'I suspected.'

'So you never had any intention of saving his life?'

'I needed information. Mr O'Keefe was a way of getting that information.' The Doctor stood up and crossed to the window that overlooked the ski slopes of SnowGlobe 6. 'I had hoped that once I got back here I could find a way of extracting the creature, reversing the damage that it had done but…'

He took a deep breath. 'The embryo Gappa is so entwined with his central nervous system that operating would have been impossible. Unfortunately, as a host he's now more dangerous than ever. The Gappa's life cycle is incredibly fast. We have to contain the creature before it hatches. So I ask again: what have you done with Mr O'Keefe?'

'He's in the morgue. Locked in one of the freezers.'

'Good.' The Doctor nodded. 'That should hold him for a while.'

'You called these things the Gappa?' said Hassan thoughtfully. 'Where do they come from?'

'From a long, long way away, Captain Hassan.' The Doctor turned, holding the Captain's gaze. 'Further than you can imagine. From a planet on the far side of the galaxy, brought here accidentally hundreds of thousands of years ago by a team of intelligent beings intent on preserving a dying race. A ship crashed. Nothing sinister, just an accident, a tragic accident. And so here it was, the last of its kind, stranded and alone on an alien planet billions of light years from home, simply trying to survive.'

Hassan pursed his thin lips. 'And you know this because…?'

'Because they told me, Captain. Because I joined my mind with theirs.'

The Doctor took a deep breath. 'And then it encountered your ancestors, and that must have been quite a meeting. Not exactly the first contact that you might have hoped.'

'My ancestors?'

'Early man! *Homo sapiens*. Flushed with success at having kicked out the Neanderthals and spoiling for a fight. Mind you, if that Gappa had turned up before they'd discovered fire then it might have been a different story.'

'Yes, fire is the most effective weapon against them.'

The Doctor's eye's narrowed. 'Something's happened, hasn't it? Tell me.'

'Oh, a lot has happened whilst you have been asleep, Doctor.' Hassan leaned back in his chair. 'And whilst your story has been fascinating speculation, allow me to furnish you with a few hard facts.'

The Doctor listened grimly as Hassan spelled out the details of the Gappa's attack on the robot maintenance workshop, of the men who had lost their lives. Eventually, teams armed with flamethrower units had driven the creatures back, and the service tunnel had been sealed with explosives.

'So all the Gappa are currently sealed in SnowGlobe 7?' The Doctor gave a nod of satisfaction. 'That's good news.'

'It would be good news, if not for the fact that the parent creature is broadcasting its telepathic signal again.'

'You seem to be well on top of that problem, Captain. Our infected patients are going to have a hard time escaping from military-issue cryo-stasis capsules.'

'Our thoughts exactly. However, those precautions are to ensure that everyone currently sheltering in SnowGlobe 6 remains secure. It is the wider implication of the creature's mental signal that is of more concern.'

The Doctor looked puzzled. 'I don't understand. You have more infected?'

Hassan gave a sharp, barking laugh. 'You could say that.'

He picked up a remote control from the desk, stabbing at the controls. A large, flat television on the wall flicked into life. A newsreader was chattering animatedly over helicopter footage of SnowGlobe 7. The Doctor stared in horror at the picture on the screen. Hundreds, maybe thousands of people swarmed around the perimeter of the dome, howling and baying like animals.

The Doctor closed his eyes. 'Martha.'

He turned to Hassan. 'How many?'

The security Captain shrugged. 'Current estimates are about two and a half thousand. The figure is rising exponentially.'

'And it will continue to rise until every creature on the

planet is infected. Hassan, you have to get me back into SnowGlobe 7. You have to get me back to my TARDIS.'

'No, Doctor. I listened to you once before, now we will deal with this ourselves.' Hassan lifted the phone on the desk. 'This is Captain Hassan. The Doctor has confirmed that fire seems to be the most effective solution. Proceed as planned.'

The Doctor leaned on Hassan's desk, staring down at the security captain.

'What are you doing, Captain?'

'The only thing we can, Doctor. Stopping this in its tracks before it spreads any further.'

'You're going to destroy the dome, aren't you?'

Hassan nodded. 'The King has authorised an air strike. A strafing run to shatter the glass dome then fuel-air bombs to destroy the creatures.'

'You can't.' Marisha was on her feet, shaking her head in disbelief. 'All those people…'

'I'm sorry. I have no choice.'

'Yes you do!' The Doctor was frantic. 'Listen to me, Captain. You don't understand what you are dealing with. The Gappa have an amazingly complicated physiological and mental profile. You can't just kill the parent creature, you will be condemning anyone infected with the dust to a life trapped inside their own minds. By the time you drop your bombs, that could be half the city! I have equipment in the TARDIS, I can break the mental hold.'

'You had your chance, Doctor, look what happened.'

'Captain, please! Get me to my TARDIS.'

'No!' Hassan slammed his hands on to the desk. 'We are

ending this now, Doctor, whether you like it or not.' He stood up, pulling his cap down hard and crossing to the door. A security guard snapped to attention.

'You are to keep the Doctor and Nurse El-Sayed in this room,' barked Hassan. 'If they attempt to leave, shoot them.'

Curtis Rabley was feeling very pleased with himself. Having escaped from the workshop, he had managed to make his way back into SnowGlobe 6 with relative ease. The security guards were more concerned with the monsters and the fire than they were with a holidaymaker in a restricted area.

He had emerged at the base of one of the ski lifts and ducked out through an access hatch, hurrying to lose himself in the agitated crowds.

His initial thought had been to get the money back into the safe, but resetting the timer would be a long and tricky operation, and so he had decided to find O'Keefe instead. The medical bay was the obvious place that they would have taken him and Rabley had worked out the perfect way of getting in there himself.

Checking that no one was watching him, he had torn the sleeve of his shirt and soaked the fabric in dark red paint from the spray can he had picked up in the maintenance bay. Rabley had always considered himself a bit of a dab hand at amateur dramatics: a few well-placed groans, coupled with his fake wound, had got him escorted to the medical bay by a couple of concerned security guards. They had even carried his holdall for him, though Rabley had to admit to a moment of panic when the soldier had taken the bag from him.

Now, standing in the lift, Rabley was running through what story he would spin O'Keefe in order to ingratiate himself with his employer again. It would have to sound plausible, though it wouldn't hurt to throw in a few instances of heroic bravery on his part.

The lift doors opened, and the guards helped Rabley out into the corridor. As they stepped into the corridor, Captain Hassan emerged from an office, his face like thunder. He cast a disapproving glance at Rabley.

'Who's this?' he snapped.

'Civilian, sir. Says he caught his arm in some machinery.'

Hassan cursed under his breath. 'We're busy up here, Private, in case you hadn't noticed!'

Rabley gave a long groan, doubling himself over.

'He seems in a bad way, sir.' The guard caught his arm.

'Very well.' Hassan waved them through impatiently. 'If they've finished in the ward, put him in there. I'll get the medic to look at him when he's got a chance.'

Hassan stepped into the lift, and Rabley allowed himself to be led down the corridor to the medical bay. He stared around in shock at the chaos. One of the guards righted a chair and pushed him down onto it.

'Sit there and keep out of the way. The medic will be along to see to you soon.'

Rabley mumbled his thanks, watching as the two guards vanished back along the corridor. As soon as they had disappeared from sight, he took a good look around the shattered remains of the medical bay. What the devil had happened to the place? It looked as though a tornado had gone through it. In the wreckage of the ward, two figures in protective clothing were checking the seals on three large coffin-like shapes. Rabley looked at them in puzzlement. What on earth was going on in here?

He ducked his head down, pretending to nurse his injured arm as the two men wheeled one of the coffins out of the ward, manhandling it over the rubble-strewn floor and easing it out down the corridor.

Rabley hurried into the ward, peering at the two remaining coffins. There was a small window set into the top of each one, the glass frosted with ice, Rabley rubbed at the glass with his sleeve. A face stared up at him. A woman.

Rabley checked the other capsule. This one held a man. He didn't recognise either of them. Could O'Keefe have been in one of the capsules that they had already wheeled away? A clipboard with a list of names had been propped up on a desk. Rabley snatched it up, running his finger down the list. O'Keefe wasn't on it.

He threw the clipboard back down. If they hadn't brought O'Keefe here, then where?

A battered silver door on the far side of the room caught his eye. It had a large sign declaring it out of bounds to all but medical personnel. Rabley rubbed his chin thoughtfully. A surgery of some kind, perhaps?

Rabley hurried over to the door. It was locked. With a quick glance down the corridor, he started to work on the lock. It was childishly easy to crack.

He eased open the door and slipped inside. The room was cold and empty. Rabley shivered. He'd been wrong. It wasn't a surgery, it was a morgue. He was about to leave when he noticed the sign pinned on one of the freezer doors. Amongst all the medical jargon he could see the name Maxwell O'Keefe written in large black letters.

Rabley stared at the sign in disbelief. After all that he'd gone through to get back in here, O'Keefe was dead after all.

'You ungrateful old wretch,' spat Rabley.

The bang from inside the freezer nearly made him jump out of his skin. The door was being rattled by something on the *inside*.

'Mr O'Keefe?' Rabley reached tentatively for the handle. 'Is that you in there, Mr O'Keefe?'

The door swung open with a heavy clunk. Tendrils of vapour curled out from the blackness. Rabley could just make out a dark shape draped in a green sheet. The sheet fluttered slightly as something moved in the darkness.

Rabley leaned closer.

'Mr O'Keefe?'

He barely had time to scream as the creature exploded out of the freezer.

NINETEEN

The guard watching the Doctor and Marisha turned white as the bloodcurdling scream rang out down the corridor. The Doctor was on his feet in a second. The guard swung his gun round to cover him. From outside, there was the sound of booted feet, muffled shouts then the rattle of gunfire.

The Doctor looked pointedly at the gun. 'Why do I get the impression that your gun might be of more use out there than in here?'

The guard hesitated, looking from the Doctor to the door and back again. More gunfire rang out from the corridor, accompanied by the familiar screams of the Gappa.

'Well don't just stand there,' snapped the Doctor. 'Find out what's going on!'

The guard eased the door open and peered into the corridor. At once, there was a barked command and he darted through the door, eyes wide with fear.

'Our cue to leave I think.' Dragging Marisha from the sofa the Doctor pushed open the office door.

Outside it was bedlam. Soldiers and security guards jostled for space, hampered by the cryo-capsule that the medical personnel were trying to get into the lift. At the far end of the corridor, the young Gappa thrashed and flailed, bellowing in rage at its tormentors.

The Doctor grimaced. 'Mr O'Keefe appears to have given birth. Come on.'

He reached for Marisha's hand, but she pulled back, shaking her head.

'You go. I'm going to be needed here.'

The Doctor's face fell. 'Are you sure?'

Marisha smiled. 'I'll be fine. Go. You said you could sort this out. Do it.'

The Doctor flashed her a dazzling smile. 'OK. See you in a bit.'

Wincing as the sound of automatic gunfire ripped through the air again, the Doctor hurled himself down the stairs.

The Doctor emerged into the foyer of the admin building, sneakers skidding on the polished marble floor.

He'd bounded down the staircase, taking the steps two or three at a time, nearly losing his balance and tumbling headlong on more than one occasion. He had practically run smack into Hassan and half a dozen soldiers, and it had only been the noise of heavy boots and Hassan's bellowed orders that had given him the time to duck through a side door as they raced past.

The birth of the young Gappa had been just what he had needed. Not only had it given him the perfect opportunity to escape, but it might also delay Hassan's air strike long enough for him to finish this once and for all.

He scanned the foyer. The once immaculate reception area was now awash with crates and military equipment. A dozen or so of the bulky cryogenic containers were lined up near the door, waiting to be loaded onto an army ambulance.

The Doctor grinned. An ambulance. Perfect. Now he just had to find a way of distracting the men in the foyer long enough to steal it.

His grin broadened as he spotted a familiar shape stacked amongst the military paraphernalia. 'There you are, Twelve. I wondered where you had got to.'

The robot had been deactivated and loaded onto a large trolley.

Pulling his sonic screwdriver from his pocket, the Doctor made a number of fine adjustments to the controls and pointed it at the motionless robot. Lights began to flicker to life across the wide metal chest, and Twelve's head straightened then turned towards the Doctor.

'Now then,' murmured the Doctor. 'Let's see if we can get you to bend a few of the rules of robotics shall we?'

He readjusted the sonic screwdriver and sent a stream of beeps and flashes towards the waiting robot. The effect was spectacular.

Service Robot Twelve tore free from the restraints sending plastic straps whipping across the reception area. Bewildered technicians and medical personnel scattered as the robot clambered to its feet, pushing through the jumble of crates and boxes and sending them flying.

The metallic voice boomed across the room.

'+DANGER! DANGER! ROBOT MUST DESTROY!+'

The personnel scrambled away as the robot stomped towards them, arms flailing wildly. A metal arm connected with one of the huge picture windows and it shattered with a deafening crash.

The Doctor darted forward, ducking though the mêlée and clambering out through the broken window and into the cab of the ambulance. He pressed the sonic screwdriver to the ignition and the engine roared into life.

Twelve was still thrashing about in the foyer, hurling crates and boxes.

The Doctor backed the ambulance up to the wrecked foyer, bellowing out of the window. 'Well come on, you great lump! Get in!'

Twelve turned and stomped over to the waiting ambulance, hauling open the rear doors and squeezing inside.

The Doctor slammed his foot on the accelerator and the ambulance shot forward.

As he navigated the winding road towards the main airlock doors, the Doctor glanced in the rear-view mirror. Twelve was staring at him and the Doctor could swear that it looked annoyed.

'+WHY DID YOU ACCESS MY VOICE UNIT AND PROGRAM THOSE WORDS?+'

'What, you've never seen *Lost in Space*? Twelve, you haven't lived.'

'+THIS UNIT IS INCAPABLE OF HARMING HUMAN BEINGS. THERE WAS NO DANGER.+'

'Yeah, but they didn't know that, did they?' The Doctor punched at a control, and the ambulance sirens blared into life, lights blazing on the roof.

He swept down towards the main airlock, swerving around anyone foolish enough to get in his way. He could see startled guards looking his way as the ambulance screeched onto the coach park and lined up with the main doors.

'Fingers crossed, Twelve. Let's see how good their emergency drill is.'

Horn blaring, the Doctor drove straight at the doors. The sentries didn't have time to think or ask for instructions, they only had time to respond. The Doctor held his breath. He was gambling that Hassan had planned to ship out the infected patients to somewhere more secure. If that was right, the guards would open the door, if not…

With a blare of klaxons, the doors swung open. The gap widened, bit by painful bit. The Doctor winced. 'This is gonna be close.'

There was a squeal of metal and a wrenching, tearing noise as one of the wing mirrors tore from the passenger-side door. The Doctor gave a whoop of delight as the ambulance shot out into the evening air, tyres squealing as he gunned the engine and sent the ambulance skidding across the car park towards SnowGlobe 7.

From the balcony of the penthouse suite, Ku'ra watched as a vehicle shot out from the doors of SnowGlobe 6 in a cloud of burning rubber and slalomed across the car park.

'Martha. Come here. Look at this.' He pointed at the careering vehicle. 'It's an ambulance. It just came out of SnowGlobe 6.'

Martha watched as the ambulance skidded out into the road, sirens blaring.

'He's driving like a madman,' said Ku'ra.

Martha nodded. 'It's a madman all right. It's the Doctor. I know it.'

'He's heading for the other dome. What's he thinking?'

'He's heading for the TARDIS.'

'Your ship? He'll never get inside the dome, there's got to be a thousand people around it.'

'He'll think of something.' Martha gripped Ku'ra's hand. 'He's the Doctor.'

It took all of the Doctor's concentration to keep from running down the hundreds of infected holidaymakers staggering in the road between the domes. Angry, snarling faces hissed at them as they passed, grasping hands swiping at the windows.

Mostly the infected people ignored them, more intent on obeying the call in their heads and reaching the dome, but every now and then a group of them would turn and spit mouthfuls of black dust at them. The Doctor flicked the windscreen wipers into life, squinting through the smeared glass as he threw the ambulance over road islands and grass verges.

'+THIS VEHICLE WAS NOT DESIGNED FOR OFF-ROAD ACTIVITIES.+'

Twelve was being thrown about in the back of the ambulance.

The Doctor shot him an angry glance in the mirror. 'Thank you, Twelve, back-seat drivers I can do without.'

'+THE CONTROL BOARDS AND SOCKETS IN THIS VEHICLE ARE COMPATIBLE WITH MY SYSTEMS IF YOU WISH ME TO TAKE CONTROL.+'

'No thanks, Twelve, I've never been a very good passenger. Now stop yakking and hang on tight.'

The Doctor swung the ambulance in a wide arc, sending it screeching into the car park of SnowGlobe 7. People scattered. They might have been possessed, but they weren't stupid enough to stand there and get run down.

The Doctor gritted his teeth as he smashed through the railings surrounding the dome. He felt a tyre burst, and the ambulance swerved alarmingly. He fought with the wheel. 'Just a few more seconds.'

The doors of SnowGlobe 7 loomed in front of them and the Doctor suddenly regretted welding them shut quite so securely.

'+DANGER. THIS VEHICLE IS IN DANGER OF COLLISION.+'

'You don't say.'

The Doctor closed his eyes as the ambulance slammed into the doors.

Martha sucked in a sharp breath as the ambulance hit the doors of the dome in a shower of sparks.

Ku'ra gave a whistle of admiration. 'Well that's one way of getting in.'

He sneezed.

'Bless you.' Martha smiled at him. Her smile faded as Ku'ra started to cough. 'Are you OK?'

'Yeah,' Ku'ra spluttered. 'I think so. Something in my throat. Dust or something—'

He stopped, staring at Martha in horror. 'Oh no…'

'Ku'ra?' Martha backed slowly away as another bout of coughing doubled Ku'ra over. Behind her, a breeze ruffled her hair. She clamped her hands over her nose.

The wind had changed direction. The dust…

'Ku'ra?'

Ku'ra straightened, his eyes wild and staring.

And lunged at her.

The Doctor groaned, pushed open the door and hauled himself out of the crumpled, battered ambulance. It had wedged itself firmly in the entranceway of SnowGlobe 7, forming almost as effective a barrier to the hordes outside as the welded doors had been.

Outside the dome, the crowds hissed and growled, the noise of hundreds of pairs of hands banging on the dome was deafening.

The Doctor leaned in through the shattered windscreen. Twelve was wedged inside the twisted wreckage 'Are you all right?'

'+MY FUNCTIONS ARE UNIMPAIRED.+'

'Can you free yourself?'

'+NOT WITHOUT CONSIDERABLE DAMAGE TO THIS VEHICLE.+'

The Doctor glanced down at the twisted bonnet. A mix

of water and oil was dripping in a steady stream onto the concrete floor.

'I wouldn't worry, I don't think that it'll be going anywhere else any time soon.'

There was a horrible, squealing wrench as the robot straightened up, peeling back the roof of the ambulance like the lid of a sardine tin. Twelve stepped from the wreckage.

The robot followed the Doctor to the airlock doors of the SnowGlobe itself. The Doctor punched at the access codes, and the doors slid open. Wind howled through the widening gap. He peered into the raging snowstorm, setting his sonic screwdriver to emit a cloaking signal. He couldn't see the TARDIS but he could sense it.

He pulled his coat tight around him and plunged into the blizzard, Twelve close behind him. He didn't bother closing the airlock doors: it didn't really matter any more. One way or another, the dome was finished.

Hassan watched as the Eurofighter swept low over the beachfront, making its sighting run on SnowGlobe 7. The sleek fighter screamed overhead then arced high into the evening air, afterburners roaring.

Hassan gave a grim smile.

A few more minutes and it would all be over.

The blizzard was getting worse. The Doctor could barely see more than a metre in front of him now, but the TARDIS was near. He could feel it.

Twelve was still right behind him, the big robot's casing

caked in snow and ice. There had been no sign of the Gappa, but the Doctor knew that they couldn't be far away. He'd been lucky. That luck only had to hold out for a few more minutes.

A familiar box-like shape suddenly emerged from the swirling snow. 'Here we go, Twelve. Home, sweet home.' The Doctor had to shout to make himself heard.

It was a mistake.

He barely had time to react as the Gappa hidden behind the TARDIS hurled itself forward. He twisted to one side, and the monster sailed over his head, claws slashing at him. It plunged into the snow, scrabbling back onto its feet, snarling and growling. The TARDIS was barely two metres away. The Doctor hunted for the key in his pocket. Could he get the door open before the creature attacked?

Hearts pounding, the Doctor spun on the balls of his feet, key gripped in his outstretched hand, ready to throw himself towards the TARDIS door.

He froze. A second Gappa was clambering over the roof of the TARDIS, thick drool splashing onto the blue painted exterior.

It launched itself at him, its hissing roar mingling with the angry cries of the one behind him as it too attacked. The Doctor dropped into the soft snow, hands clasped over his head, waiting for the feel of claws and teeth.

The blows never came. With an electronic bellow, Twelve lunged forward catching the Gappa in mid air. The Doctor looked up. The robot stood over him, arms outstretched, a squealing, thrashing monster held in each hand. There were a series of sickening pops as each huge metal fist closed tight and thick black ichor sprayed into the frigid air.

Twelve dropped the two twisted corpses into the bloodstained snow, then reached down and hauled the Doctor to his feet.

'Thank you, Twelve,' said the Doctor solemnly.

'+THERE ARE MORE LIFE SIGNS CONVERGING ON THIS AREA.+'

'Then we should get inside.'

The Doctor unlocked the TARDIS. Twelve bent almost double and squeezed himself through the police-box doors. The Doctor followed him inside.

Shrugging off his coat and throwing it in the general direction of the hatstand, the Doctor hurried over to the central console. Twelve stood motionless inside the doors, processors whirring frantically.

'+SENSORS INDICATE THAT INTERNAL VOLUME OF THIS SPACE IS NOT CONSISTANT WITH ITS EXTERNAL DIMENSIONS.+'

'If you mean it's bigger on the inside, why don't you just say so?'

'+THIS DOES NOT COMPUTE.+'

'No. Good isn't it? Now be quiet, eh? Got a little bit to do and not much time to do it.'

The Doctor's hands flew over the TARDIS controls. He darted manically from one segment of the console to the next, checking readings, setting search programs in motion, calibrating dials and settings with complex precision. Slowly, a deep bass throbbing started to build deep within the bowels of the time machine, a vibration that set the floor panels rattling and shaking dust from the great coral beams that arced over the console.

Finally, the Doctor stopped, peering at the monitor screen, nodding to himself in quiet satisfaction. Everything was set. He placed his hand over an innocuous little switch on the console. He concentrated, linking his mind with the telepathic controls of the TARDIS, focusing on the thousands of people outside the dome.

And pressed the switch.

Hassan stared open-mouthed at his television monitor as the crowd surrounding SnowGlobe 7 dropped to the floor in unison. Several thousand people falling silently as one.

In the penthouse suite of the Burj Al-Arab hotel, a sudden dazed expression crossed Ku'ra's face and, with a wistful smile, he collapsed onto the thick carpet.

Martha was about to kneel down to check his pulse when a blaze of brilliant white light lit up the evening sky.

High over Dubai, the pilot of the Eurofighter turned his head away from the glare as the entire glass dome of SnowGlobe 7 lit up from within like an enormous light bulb. Glass panels of the dome started to crack and craze and, with a mighty roar, the roof of the dome exploded outwards on a billowing cloud of steam.

Eyes streaming from the light, the pilot broke off his attack run, sending the fighter screaming away from the vast vapour cloud.

***

Deep in the ice of SnowGlobe 7, the Gappa felt its link with the minds of its prey severed moments before the wave of blazing heat blasted through the cavern. Ice turned to steam in a matter of seconds and, with a last defiant cry of rage and pain, the last of the Gappa was vaporised.

TWENTY

Martha moved slowly through the thousands of dazed and confused patients who were slowly coming to their senses in the car park of SnowGlobe 7. Medical personnel were everywhere, treating those that had injured themselves as they fell, taking blood samples to check for evidence of contamination by the black dust. It was the same all over the city. Everyone who had been infected by the dust was free of the creature's influence, totally unable to remember anything of the last few dreadful hours.

Martha had stopped to help where she could, checking on those with cuts and bruises, helping those still regaining consciousness to their feet and pointing them in the direction of help.

She had left Ku'ra in one of the beds in the penthouse suite of the hotel. She would go back and check that he was all right later. He seemed unhurt and it was as comfortable a place as any. Besides, Cowley had paid for the room, and she certainly wasn't going to be needing it.

She had found the Director's body at the base of the hotel. She had alerted a nearby paramedic team and they had made arrangements to have the body taken care of. Martha wished that she had been able to do something for Director Cowley, but she had underestimated the depth of the creature's hold over her; either that or she had underestimated Cowley's single-minded desire for her SnowGlobe project to succeed. In the end, Martha had decided that she would prefer to believe it was the malign influence of the creature in the ice that had been responsible for Cowley's urge to commit genocide, not her blind ambition. That was no way for anyone to be remembered.

Besides, what would Cowley have said if she could have seen the state of her precious SnowGlobe? Martha stared up at the steaming wreckage of the shattered dome. The billowing geyser of steam had gone on for what seemed like hours. Even now, a fine spray continued to fall on the bewildered city. Summer rain in Dubai. Martha shook her head. Only with the Doctor...

She ducked under the hazard tape that soldiers were starting to put up around the dome and squeezed past the wreck of the ambulance that had been winched free of the doors. Inside, glass covered everything. The massive airlock doors had been blown clear across the foyer, and Martha could see sky through the huge, jagged hole in the dome.

She clambered through the remains of the airlock and picked her way carefully through the piles of broken glass. Where previously there had been snow and ice and raging winds, there was now only wet, steaming rock. In the distance, she could see the familiar police-box shape of the TARDIS. The Doctor was standing outside it, hands thrust deep into his pockets, staring up at the evening sky.

Glass crunching underfoot, Martha hurried over to him. He looked down as she approached, his lean face breaking into a dazzling smile.

'Martha Jones! Am I glad to see you.' He threw his arms around her and gave her a huge hug.

Martha hugged him back. 'Sorry, Doctor.'

He looked at her, puzzled. 'Sorry? What for?'

'You left me to look after Cowley. I let her escape. Let her cause all this.'

'I'm not sure that you'd have been able to do much to stop Miss Cowley. From the little I knew of her, she was quite a formidable lady, and coupled with the psychic influence of the Gappa...'

'Gappa?' Martha raised a quizzical eyebrow. 'Is that what they were called?'

The Doctor nodded sadly. 'The last of their kind.'

'And you wanted to save them.'

'I thought I could.' The Doctor thrust his hands back into his pockets, kicking at the rock with his trainers. 'I wanted to try and stop another race from vanishing from the universe, but the universe had already decided that it was their time to die.'

He looked at Martha with sadness in his eyes. 'The Gappa should never have survived, they should all have been dead a hundred thousand years ago. Their life cycle was a biological dead end, an aberration of evolution.

It was only the good intentions of another species that allowed them to cheat death, a well-meaning preservation effort that could have meant the end of all life on Earth.'

'And is that what this was?' Martha looked around the dome. 'A well-meaning preservation effort by a doomed species?'

'Nah.' The Doctor shook his head. 'This is human beings doing what they do best, surviving. Adapting. Confronting problems head-on. It's me who should be apologising to you. It's me that's ruined it. Millions of tonnes of Arctic ice, boiled away in an instant.'

'Yes, and how did you manage that exactly?'

'Like I said, a well-meaning preservation effort. The Gappa was being transported from its home planet to be preserved in some kind of zoo or safari park or something. But they never got there. They crashed.'

'On Earth?'

'Yup.'

'In the past.'

'In the Stone Age.'

'Hence the cave paintings.'

'Exactly! You were lucky. If the Gappa had managed to wipe out *Homo sapiens*, you lot would never have got off the first rung of civilisation. You'd just be another doomed world twirling towards extinction.'

Martha shivered. The wind was starting to pick up again. 'So these well-meaning scientists that crashed. That means there was a spacecraft, right?'

The Doctor nodded. 'Right. A great big state-of-the-art starship, with a state-of-the-art plasma fusion drive buried in the ice of the prehistoric Arctic since the last Ice Age. Well, I say that. Most of it is probably still up there. They came in pretty hard. Ship broke into a dozen pieces or more.'

'But the engine ended up here?'

'Frozen in the same ice as the Gappa.'

'And you blew it up.'

'Used the TARDIS scanner to track down the fusion core. A hundred thousand years in the ice and still enough fuel to go critical. Masses of heat, no fallout. Good thing I found it, not you lot. They can be very dangerous in the wrong hands.'

Martha stared at him. Despite the flippancy of his comments, there was a deep sadness in the Doctor's eyes. He had hated destroying the Gappa. In the end, it had come down to a simple choice. Gappa or human. Kill or be killed. Thank God he was on their side.

She squeezed his arm. 'Do you know who they were then, these good Samaritans who crashed a hundred thousand years ago?'

The Doctor shook his head. 'Not a clue.'

'Wanna go and find out?'

The Doctor beamed at her. 'Martha Jones, you're a woman after my own heart.'

Martha was about to point out how true that comment was when she was distracted by the sight of a huge robot squeezing out through the TARDIS doors.

'What?'

'Ah, Martha, meet Twelve. Twelve, this is my best friend, Martha Jones.'

'+PLEASED TO MEET YOU, MISS JONES.+'

Martha started at the robot, momentarily dumbstruck.

She looked at the Doctor in disbelief. 'Surely we're not taking him with us?'

The Doctor's face fell. After the stress of the last few hours, the Doctor's hurt-little-boy expression was more than Martha could take.

She burst out laughing.

Martha perched on an outcrop of lichen-covered rock and watched though the Doctor's high-tech opera glasses as the group of hunters swathed in thick fur made their way slowly through the thick snow, heading south, following the mammoth herd, searching for food on the tundra.

She lowered the glasses and smiled, amazed – not for the first time – by how quickly she had got used to something as mind-boggling as being able to wander though her own prehistory.

The Doctor had programmed Twelve with a series of instructions for Mr Roberts on how to rebuild the robots' memory and a farewell message for Marisha. Martha had been sad not to have a chance to say a proper goodbye but, as the Doctor had pointed out, they had just been responsible for the destruction of a major government scientific facility and that might not make them the most popular people on the planet.

She raised the glasses again, focusing on the tiny figure far below her. The Doctor was making his final sweep through the remains of the crashed spacecraft that had brought the Gappa to prehistoric Earth.

She and the Doctor had arrived earlier in the day, watching as the stricken craft had arced through the air like a fiery comet, clipping the top of the distant glacier in a gout of flame and ploughing nose-first into the valley below. The spacecraft had broken into a dozen pieces, just as the Doctor had predicted, the section housing the engines and the Gappa skidding to a halt on the ice sheet below them.

They had watched from the safety of the TARDIS as the alien had crawled through the wreckage and slowly made its way through the snow towards the glacier, and the future.

The Doctor had identified the ship as Modrakanian. As the sun had started to rise, he had left Martha on the top of the hill with his opera glasses, told her to watch and taken the TARDIS on a brief trip down into the valley.

As the sun had cleared the distant mountains, Martha had watched spellbound as the mammoth herd shook the last vestiges of the night's snow from their fur and, snorting and bellowing, began the long journey south.

A more familiar bellowing echoed up from the valley, and the tiny, distant shape of the TARDIS faded away, reappearing a few seconds later alongside her.

The Doctor emerged, following Martha's gaze towards the distant mammoths and the hunters that tracked them.

'Fancy a mammoth steak for dinner?'

Martha grimaced. 'No, thank you!'

'Good for you. Puts hair on your chest.'

'Definitely no, then.' She clambered to her feet. 'Did you find them?'

The Doctor nodded solemnly. He had been determined to find the bodies of the crew of the doomed Modrakanian ship, to take them back home to their own planet for a proper burial. Martha guessed it was his way of making up for failing to save the Gappa.

'So, I guess its Modrakania next stop?'

'Yes!' The Doctor rubbed his hands together briskly. 'And then, if you don't mind, I'd like to go somewhere where they've never heard of snow.'

Martha pulled her parka around her. 'That's fine by me.'

The Doctor pushed open the TARDIS door and ushered Martha inside,

'Where did you have in mind?' she asked.

'Ever heard of Western-super-Mare?'

The door slammed closed. Moments later a rasping alien trumpeting echoed round the valley. A lone mammoth, straggling behind the herd, bellowed in reply, but the TARDIS had gone.

Acknowledgements

Once again I am hugely indebted to Justin Richards for his constant faith and encouragement, as well as his endless patience when my effects work starts to get in the way of my writing.

Hugs to Pam Tucker and Sue Cowley for proofreading, spellchecking and the general tidying up of this book.

Thanks also to the usual suspects who have to put up with me when I have a deadline looming and have made the last year that much nicer by their presence.

Karen Parks

Steve Roberts

Steve Cole

Andy Tucker

Nick Kool

Nick Sainton-Clark

Peter Tyler

And to David and Freema, without whom…